Christmas in Paris 2002

Christmas in Paris 2002

BY
RONALD K. FRIED

THE PERMANENT PRESS
Sag Harbor, New York 11963

Library of Congress Cataloging-in-Publication Data

Fried, Ronald K., 1955-
    Christmas in Paris, 2002 / by Ronald K. Fried.
        p.   cm.
    ISBN 1-57962-114-7
        1. United States—Foreign public opinion, French—Fiction.
    2. Americans—France—Fiction. 3. Paris (France)—Fiction. I. Title.

PS3606.R55C48 2005
813'.6—dc22   2005050955

Printed in The United States of America.

For L

"Human society is like the ocean: it resumes its normal level and rhythm after a cataclysm, and obliterates all traces of it by the ebb and flow of its voracious interests."

—Honoré de Balzac, *A Murky Business*

⁕ ONE ⁕

They emerged into Paris, as they always did, with a view of the faintly yellow, nineteenth-century apartment building where Joseph Steiner had lived as a student. Its distinct tint set it apart from the grayish but equally elegant structures around it. The building faced the Metro station in the sixth arrondissement neighborhood where Steiner and his wife stayed during what had become their annual visits. As the escalator carried them up to street level, Steiner searched for the window of the bedroom that had been his almost thirty years earlier. His shifting perspective brought to mind a crane shot in a movie when the camera rises toward the heavens, inviting the audience to take the long view, think a significant thought. Though Steiner worked in television, a visual medium, he held onto the old-fashioned prejudice that film was imprecise compared to the written word. Steiner liked to boast that he and Mary rarely went to the movies anymore, though Mary warned that this just made them sound old.

As they reached the street, Steiner gestured toward his former sixth-story window with its small black Arabesque wrought iron balcony.

"That's exactly where I lived," Steiner said.

"That's exactly what you say every time we do this," Mary replied.

Steiner felt duly chastised—but for what? Repetitiveness? Soft-headed nostalgia? Aren't those among the very reasons Americans visit Paris? Well, the time for sentimental European holidays certainly seemed to have passed. And Steiner knew Mary was right: he did repeat himself. Besides, insular concerns about his small self didn't seem appropriate at the current historical moment, with almost daily arrests of terrorists in Paris and its suburbs, and war in Iraq penciled in on the world's calendar for a few months hence. It was Christmas of 2002; why dwell on his own parochial story when history was being violently written everywhere? Steiner's solipsistic worldview seemed worse than out of vogue: even to Steiner it felt like blindness. Yet his own story is likely what he would be contemplating if the towers of history down-crashed on his head.

It was impossible for Steiner to take that first step on the Parisian sidewalk and not wonder what his twenty-year-old self, only a year older than his own son Michael, would have made of the forty-nine-year-old Steiner who now flattered himself to think that he displayed a measure of cosmopolitan confidence as he walked toward the Boulevard Saint Germain with one tightly edited bag of overpriced but not inelegant clothing slung over his shoulder.

When Steiner came here as a college student in 1975, Paris, of course, seemed entirely interesting to his young eyes—from the tiny antique-looking Citroëns to the way the women, who used so much more make-up than American girls, wore their long tight sweaters pulled down under their short leather jackets. But by now the journey across the ocean seemed no more extraordinary than a trip from Steiner's apartment on the East Side of Manhattan to the West Side where he was raised. Perhaps, to voice the familiar complaint, the world had become homogenous with the same stores, food, clothing, and movies showing up everywhere. Or maybe, Steiner feared, his youthful, highly charged interest in Parisian life was fading along with his virility, his eyesight, his physical allure. His recent habit of dwelling on his age began as a ploy, a way of inviting the young people who worked for him to say he didn't look his age. But lately Steiner felt a shift: he was no longer pretending to be old; he was *becoming* old. And something within him wanted to hasten the transition.

"This place is great," Steiner told the very young woman who had waited around to give him the keys to the apartment that he and Mary were borrowing from friends. Steiner felt himself smiling as he must have the first time he stepped into one of the great Parisian cafés almost three decades ago—smiling as if being in a beautiful place where important men had been would somehow make his own life beautiful or important. This was a pathetic fallacy, he knew even then. Still, his friends' apartment was lovely with its southern exposure and view of the Boulevard Saint Germain, which took on a quiet bourgeois charm in the seventh arrondissement. He'd visited the place before, but now it was to be his and Mary's for the next ten days. Why shouldn't Steiner grin a big dopey American grin?

One of Steiner's absent hosts was in a place where there'd just been a war, while the other was on her way to a place where war was coming soon. Tad Wheeler was a TV news producer who'd been sent to Afghanistan, while Tad's wife Judith, a newspaper reporter, was headed back to Saddam Hussein's Baghdad where she'd been assigned for most of the previous month. Steiner had just lost what Tad called the "big corporate job" Steiner held for five years in New York. Steiner had received a decent severance package; and because Mary was the proprietor of a small publishing house, she could set her own schedule. So they really had no excuse not to take the offer to spend Christmas in Tad and Judith's six-room apartment in the heart of the precious, affluent center of Paris, a city done up for the holidays with the sort of restrained good taste that could only be developed over centuries.

Dominique, the girl who had given Steiner the key, had news: Judith was still in Paris. Problems with her visa had delayed her departure until the next day. Judith would be back at the apartment at eight, Dominique said. "She invites you to join her for dinner with her friends."

The young woman lingered in the entryway, as if she wanted something else. On the wall behind her was an African mask Judith had picked up while on assignment. The apartment, Steiner knew from his previous visits, was almost entirely decorated with souvenirs from some of the most dangerous places in the world: the carved wooden base of the glass coffee table in the living room had been a child's bed in Ethiopia; the rug beneath it came from Kabul.

Dominique's tight hip-hugging jeans with flared legs looked like the jeans that girls wore when Steiner was in high school. The style was still prevalent when he'd come to Paris for the first time. Was that a peasant blouse she was wearing? That's what they were called when Steiner was sixteen and their hint of transparency contributed to the boner he seemed to have throughout his high school career. Those were the days. While Steiner at first rebelled at the revival of so many styles

9

from his youth, he now found something pleasantly nostalgic about seeing the old looks again: it connected his middle-aged libido to its younger, more insistent iteration.

Mary would know if the phrase "peasant blouse" had survived. She worked at a fashion magazine when Steiner first met her, and she was currently the best-dressed left-wing publisher in Manhattan. Perhaps she was even the best-dressed left-wing publisher in the world, though there likely weren't many contenders for the title.

Dominique worked for Tad. Brunette, freckled, blue-eyed, her English was so good that it made Steiner feel renewed shame for his less-good French, as well as the deep inadequacies of his almost elite American education. The girl wanted to work in New York, and Tad had evidently told her that Steiner was a successful executive there. True enough. That is exactly what Steiner *was*, as in used to be a month ago, but the feeling of being in power was fading fast. When you lose your job, you find out just how conventional you are—to what extent you judge yourself in the same way that the least sympathetic stranger might judge you at a cocktail party.

After Steiner told Dominique to send him her reel, she offered a walking tour of the sixth arrondissement.

"Oh, I know it quite well," he said. "We visit at least once a year, and I lived down the street in 1975."

"She wasn't born yet," Mary told Steiner, as a way of instructing him to stop flirting.

"That's right," the girl said with a laugh, and then she was off.

Steiner did not think he'd actually been flirting. Dominique was maybe two years older than his son, so she was not yet entirely a woman in his eyes. Part of Steiner wished Michael were here with them now. The trip he took with Michael to Paris and London three years earlier was the best time father and son had had together in years. Steiner showed off his knowledge of the cities, Paris particularly. Turn left, turn right, here we are, just like I told you, this is the Places des Vosges. I know that café over there. The food isn't bad, if you're hungry. We can have oysters. I'll let you order a glass of wine. Michael seemed impressed for perhaps the last time before he assumed his dour adolescent duty and began to disparage everything his father did.

"He's even better at it than you are," Steiner told Mary some time near Michael's senior year in high school, and part of Steiner was—without a trace of irony—pissed off that mother and son seemed united in their mocking emasculation, though Steiner and his mother had done the same thing to Steiner's father.

In Tad and Judith's living room now, Mary was speaking to Michael on the international cell phone she'd purchased despite her husband's complaints that it was unnecessary. Michael was up early to finish writing one last paper at that disturbingly arty, cripplingly expensive college for bohemian children of privilege who couldn't quite make it into the Ivy League.

"You'll have to ask your father," Mary said with a quick wink as she handed Steiner the expensive phone he was now glad they had with them.

"I didn't know you had to write papers at that school," Steiner said.

"That joke wasn't funny the first time you tried it, Dad," Michael said, before asking if his friends could stay in the apartment when they came to town for an anti-war demonstration.

"How many kids?"

"Just a couple."

"How many?" Steiner asked again.

"Really, just a few," Michael said, as Steiner imagined a dozen unclean, latter-day hippies picking at their naked toes on his sofa and having inexpert but enthusiastic sexual intercourse in every room of the apartment. He thought of Michael's new girlfriend—what was her name?—with her pretty but unshaven legs. Steiner didn't really want anyone staying in his home except his son, but he gave his permission. You can't be a schmuck to your own son, even though you sometimes would like to be.

"Don't trash the place," Steiner warned on the phone, though he knew Michael might miss his irony.

"Dad," Michael said, "that absolutely won't happen."

This sounded a bit patronizing, but perhaps Michael was merely being sincere.

Many young people, even those who used to work for Steiner, didn't even look him in the eye when answering a direct question. But Michael still looked everyone in the eye, and unlike many of his friends, he spoke from his heart. And the pot smoking that Michael and his fellow protestors would do in the apartment didn't really bother Steiner all that much. Intoxication was also a teacher.

During their vacation together, Michael asked his father to name the biggest mistake he had made while living in Paris as a student. "A glass or two of wine with dinner would have been a good idea," Steiner confessed. "It would have loosened me up."

And what did Steiner drink with his solitary dinners in Paris when he was twenty years old? Water. Yes, water. What a horrible choice that was. Steiner went to the same inexpensive storefront restaurant each night, waited in line not speaking to the French students or the Germans or even the Americans, ordered his *carrot rappé*, his *poulet roti* and *pommes de terres*, and asked for a fucking glass of water? He still remembered the phrase, *eau robinet*, tap water. *Une carafe d'eau.*

Steiner winced at the thought. A carafe of water. One night, the balding Basque waiter with the broad shoulders brought Steiner a glass of milk, claiming it's what he thought Steiner had asked him for. Steiner was convinced, convinced to this day, that the waiter served the milk just to embarrass the young American who ate dinner by himself on most nights, always ordering water with his meal, but never ordering a glass of milk because absolutely no one in the Western World over the age of eight drank milk with their dinner. No, not even back then was Steiner's French so bad that he'd attempt to say "*l'eau*" and have it come out "*lait.*"

That's one awful little story he would never tell Mary. It was just too stupidly painful. He had, however, often told Mary about when, as a twenty-year-old student, he'd decided spontaneously over a coffee at the Café de la Mairie on Saint Sulpice that it was a mistake not to flirt with the large-breasted German student, the girl who insisted on speaking to him in her extremely good English at a time when Steiner had vowed to speak only French. Steiner and the girl had often ended up sitting near each other at the front of the café on spring afternoons when Steiner stopped in on his way back from class. The girl smiled at Steiner and spoke to him at least once a week. Steiner had wanted to have a French girlfriend while he was in Paris, but it was getting late in the year. In only a few months, he'd return to the States, as he'd come to call

12

America, and here was a pretty girl who talked *to him*. In English. And she was European, after all, a German, which was closer to being French than American. So what if Steiner, a Jew from West End Avenue—whose own father had fought the Germans—was raised by parents who habitually used the phrase, "goddamned Krauts"? Only a frightened fool would turn Gitta away. With her upturned nose and long brown hair, she seemed, however, not his type, and Steiner, having read his Proust, worried about the dangers of throwing his life away for a woman who wasn't his type. But this was just another idea misappropriated from a literary masterpiece, distorted and turned into an excuse not to live life.

It was fairly easy to get Gitta to laugh when Steiner made the concession he'd vowed not to make: he answered in English when he was addressed in English. The invitation to Gitta's sunless little room on the rue des Notre Dames des Champs came less than a week later with the same ease with which he took her hand as they walked south towards the Luxembourg Gardens in the chilly April rain, as easily as Gitta removed her heather Shetland wool sweater, grabbed the top of Steiner's jeans, expressed mild surprise that he was circumcised, and briefly demonstrated her gift for fellatio before producing a condom and then settling down for what in retrospect seemed like first-rate sexual intercourse. Steiner didn't dare touch those impressive white breasts for fear that he'd come right away and disappoint the intelligent, good-natured girl from Munich who thus far in their sexual encounter seemed generous and patient. She was a student at the École des Beaux Arts. On the dusty floor next to her bed were neat stacks of French language art history books arranged in chronological order. On the top of the pile nearest the bed was a book about postwar American art featuring a Jasper Johns American Flag painting on its cover. Next to the art books were copies of *Der Spiegel*. President Gerald Ford grinned earnestly from the cover of the most recent edition. This, together with the Johns' flag, gave Steiner's first-ever Parisian sexual success an air of patriotic triumph. The distracting sight of the dull President helped the young Steiner delay his climax briefly until Gitta, saying something in German above him, became the first woman to experience a loud and seemingly fulsome orgasm while having intercourse with Steiner. Steiner was

13

impressed, not so much with his own fledgling performance, but with the girl's abandon, the volume of her cries. He was impressed with everything about Gitta, and he was impressed with his own dumb good luck, too—good luck that he'd been so close to squandering.

As Steiner prepared for the acrobatic challenge of taking what passed for a shower in Tad and Judith's tiny Parisian tub, he came face to face with his friends' entirely humbling careers. Their bathroom was a dauntingly impressive photo gallery: dawn in Nairobi; a market in Peking; Tad smiling amid a crowd of exuberant school children in newly liberated Kuwait. Captions pencilled in elegant script below each photo explained where and when the pictures had been taken.

Tad and Judith's professional resumes were a litany of disasters: floods, famines, train wrecks, hostage situations, and the like. Plus diplomatic goings-on in Brussels, Frankfurt, the Elysée Palace. Steiner's friends had worked in every hellish, troubled corner of the world, while Steiner could only summon the energy for a yearly visit to Paris and perhaps one other Western European city. Just crossing the Atlantic in coach upset Steiner's delicate system. Hong Kong, Tokyo—Steiner had never seen them. He had never ventured into the Third World, except for one trip to a luxury resort in the middle of an impoverished Caribbean island, which just made him feel like shit. Mary did better. Once a year or so, she was off to Africa or Central America to meet with writers or publishers. She'd been to Cuba on business several times. Steiner always declined her invitations to come along. He didn't relish feeling like someone's spouse, someone with nothing better to do than go shopping, sit around the pool, or look at churches he'd soon forget. The job Steiner had just lost had allowed him only three weeks of vacation each year. In the spring, he and Mary spent a week in Western Europe, while each summer they spent the last two weeks of August at their weekend home in Connecticut. But when you're out of work, you're out of excuses not to do the things you don't want to do. So Steiner was out of excuses to not at least pretend to want to grow, to use one of Mary's pet words. He might even have to accompany her to the Frankfurt Book Fair next fall. There was an incentive to find a job as quickly as possible.

But Tad, Tad was doing a lot better than Steiner. Tad was five years younger, spoke much better French, and had spent the previous seven years traveling the world. He said his Arabic was now passable. Arabic? How did Tad learn Arabic? Half the time Steiner couldn't understand the numbers the cashier rattled off at a Parisian supermarket. But Tad was still hustling all over the planet like an aging athlete who kept on learning new moves despite the aches and pains, the muscle pulls, and the bruised bones he'd taught himself to ignore.

Now, of course, Steiner felt like he had no profession, while Tad, as an American war correspondent, was a part of a great new growth industry.

Tad was among the first American journalists in Kabul after the Taliban fell, and he was slated to be in Southern Iraq in February or March of 2003—which is when everyone guessed the war would begin. Tad's wife would be there, too. Both were currently negotiating with their bosses at the international media corporations that employed them to make sure that they'd be assigned to the same theater of combat. "Otherwise," Judith had reported to Steiner via e-mail, "Tad and I won't see each other for months." Especially if you get killed, Steiner thought.

Steiner himself had only once heard the sound of distant gunfire. He was passing Tompkins Square Park on the Lower East Side where Mary lived before they were married, and he heard the pop-pop of a handgun. By the time he reached the front door of Mary's apartment building on the south end of the park, police cars with wailing sirens and flashing lights were converging at the corner he'd just passed.

"It's really time to move out of here," he told her.

"You're so bourgeois," Mary replied.

Yes, she was absolutely right, though Steiner was not nearly as well-born as his future wife with her often-broke, often-drunk, almost-renowned painter father and shabby genteel mother whose own parents had been listed in the *Social Register*.

While Mary served her time on the Lower East Side—back when the neighborhood was a genuinely dangerous crack-and-heroin emporium—she was like a trust fund kid who knew that in a crisis daddy's money could come to the rescue. Not that her family actually *had* any money, it was just that everyone they *knew* had money—which often felt like the same thing: it made her somehow safe, somehow entitled. Steiner, whose parents had more money but were not nearly as well-connected in social or artistic circles, thought he understood this about his wife better than she did—largely because Mary denied it. Family friends had always treated Mary as a special case because of her parents' struggles. Growing up, she spent time in other people's houses in the Hamptons, Provence, Tuscany, places that Steiner wouldn't get his eyes on until much later, after they'd been overexposed like movie stars who did too much TV.

Together with almost everyone he grew up with on West End Avenue, Steiner was deeply and unapologetically middle class. And when it came to physical violence, he was a coward, too—just like everyone else. Which is why Steiner was unreservedly pleased when he saw a young Arab man being carefully searched by security at JFK as he and Mary boarded their plane to Paris twelve hours earlier. "Racial profiling works," friends in New York now said with a guiltless smirk, experiencing none of the liberal qualms they would have felt if they'd said the same thing eighteen months earlier. The disaster that had come to be known simply as 9/11 gave many of Steiner's friends a convenient excuse for a political shift they'd felt coming anyway as they got a bit richer, paid more taxes, and succumbed—like Steiner himself—to a deepening fear of an impoverished old age, terrorist attacks, foreigners, a renewed crime wave, any aesthetic blight upon their beloved wealthy Manhattan.

While many said that the attack on the World Trade Center would change them, few did change. Courageous people—firemen and cops and ordinary people, too—behaved courageously. But Steiner cringed as TV transformed this genuine heroism into kitsch heroism, though there was nothing new there, as readers of Kundera understood. The New Yorkers Steiner knew, however, weren't heroic, and the attack just made them more like themselves. He'd seen it at the office. Lazy people retreated into paralysis; hard-working people made themselves busier; angry people got angrier; and those who tended to feel sorry for themselves experienced the calamity as something that had happened to them, even if they were miles away from the disaster, were not physically harmed, and knew no one who was killed or rendered homeless.

16

After 9/11, Mary, too, had done what she always did: she quickly published a book. The independent press Mary ran put out a small list of no more than thirty books each year. They were mostly left-wing political books, surprisingly popular works of Jungian psychology, and translations of novels by Third World writers. One of the latter had recently been short-listed for the Nobel Prize for novels set in Africa. Where exactly in Africa? Steiner wasn't sure. He couldn't retain it, just as he couldn't remember the names of the flowers Mary patiently pointed out in the garden of their country home each spring. Some things stuck in his brain, and some things didn't. Zambia? No, that wasn't it. Steiner hadn't read a word the African author had written. In fact, he'd never read a word that any African author had ever written. Steiner knew that this was wrong, just as he was surely wrong years earlier when he opposed Mary's publishing enterprise.

"I totally lack the entrepreneurial spirit that made America great," he told her after the company became something of a success.

"I wouldn't brag about that if I were you," she said.

Mary was right again when she saw that women throughout America would purchase seemingly impenetrable Jungian analyses of unhappy families, psychological dysfunction. And she was right when she e-mailed one of her well-known former professors to urge him to write a short history of Islamic radicalism from the perspective of an unrepentant left-winger.

"This really proves that America is one of the worst countries in the world," the professor said when Steiner picked up the telephone in his Connecticut home a few days after the 9/11 attack.

"I'll give you to Mary," was all Steiner said in reply. Though he was deeply offended, Steiner understood that starting an argument would be bad for Mary's business. Besides, the man on the phone was a professional advocate, so Steiner would doubtless lose the debate anyway.

Mary's professor didn't want to write the book, Steiner gathered as he overheard his wife's conversation while he opened a bottle of white Burgundy. But the celebrated and naïve political zealot was no match for Mary's willful, worldly charm.

"Stop thinking so much and just write this book," Mary said into the phone as she smiled and took a glass of wine from Steiner.

Though Steiner had never met Mary's "crazy father," as she always called him, Steiner guessed that he heard an echo of the father's bossy, privileged tone when Mary bullied or hectored one of her authors into doing precisely what she wished. It was a voice she'd used countless times to make Michael write a paper he'd been putting off.

Mary rushed the professor's short book into print, and it became a modest international success. It had recently been quoted on the front page of *Le Monde*. Mary sold the sub rights all over the world, and the profits would fund her publishing house for at least a year. Michael had read the book in galleys, and he caused a small sensation at his college when Mary brought her author to lecture there. "It was great, Dad," Michael reported on the phone from school that night. "He got a standing ovation. You definitely should have come. Mom took us out to dinner and my political theory professor came."

Before Steiner and Mary took off for Paris, they saw a copy of the thin paperback near the checkout counter at a bookstore at JFK.

"You're the only person I know who benefited from 9/11," Steiner said.

Mary looked so offended that Steiner thought for a moment that she might refuse to go to Paris.

"I'll buy you a copy if you read it on the plane," she said instead of losing her temper.

Steiner declined politely.

Steiner prided himself on his ability—rare among American males, he liked to think—to bathe in a tiny space with a portable showerhead without soaking an entire bathroom. And it bothered him that Mary never sufficiently praised this skill. After making sure that he had indeed managed not to spray water all over the international photo gallery that was his friends' Parisian *salle de bain*, Steiner felt too awake to begin the nap he and Mary always permitted themselves after crossing the Atlantic. No, a short walk—and maybe an early afternoon drink—were in order.

On the way into the bedroom, Steiner paused in front of a picture of a teenage boy in Arab robe and headdress. The boy, seated on dusty ochre earth, his back leaning against a stucco wall, smiled a proud, secretive half-smile. In his left hand, he held a thin, elaborately decorated, delicate-looking object. It might have been a musical instrument, lovingly painted with cheerful geometric patterns in bright reds, yellows, and greens, all set off by a white background. If Steiner found a rug or pillow with that pattern, he'd buy it for his summer home. Was the boy holding a wind instrument of some kind? Steiner leaned in. It was a weapon, a Kalasknikov, if Steiner didn't miss his guess.

But then again, what did he know about firearms?

The couple who lived in this apartment worked in what Steiner had been trained to call the real world. They were professional witnesses to the nightmare of history from which Steiner, taught to follow Joyce's Stephen Dedalus, was trying to awake, though these days history was just too insistent—and too dangerous—to ignore.

When Steiner woke up in the morning in New York, he read the *Times* with an intensity that Mary pronounced Talmudic, meaning that he concentrated on the paper with the fervor his ancestors had lavished upon religious texts. If he hadn't gotten enough sleep, he was forced to use his reading glasses, but he tried to do without them. On the subway going to and from work, Steiner read Balzac. He picked up the habit four years earlier after reading *Le Père Goriot* during one exhilarating rainy weekend in the country. Until then, Balzac was one of the many gaps in Steiner's liberal education. Mary said that the Balzac mania was fueled by Steiner's unconscious desire to avoid reading the books she published. Maybe she had a point. Maybe it was a conscious desire. There had been a time he dutifully read all of Mary's books. But Steiner was much more at home with Balzac's striving, scheming, selfish early nineteenth-century Paris than among Mary's Third World fiction writers, her plaintive left wingers, or her Jungian seekers of in-depth psychological wisdom.

Steiner was reasonably sure that he'd read every volume of Balzac available in English translation. He made his way through some of the shorter, easier books in French after he'd first read them in English, keeping the English version at hand for use when he was stumped. He now preferred inexhaustible, chatty, ham-fisted, melodramatic Balzac to Joyce's favorite—exquisite, artful, controlled Flaubert. Balzac could move from the gutter outside an impoverished boarding house to the mansions of the Faubourg Saint Germain, which were not far from where Steiner would be spending the next ten days. Balzac knew the prisons, gambling dens, whorehouses, theaters, and newspaper offices. He knew the police, lawyers, spies, ministers, moneylenders, and pawnbrokers. Balzac understood money. He was the ideal novelist for someone like Steiner who'd spent the last five years working for a large American corporation.

Steiner never talked books with Mary's literary friends. He was a mere TV executive, and they took him seriously only when they solicited his help promoting their books on television. When Mary's writers sought Steiner's advice on their TV appearances, he felt condescended to—as if he were the good-natured, stay-at-home wife of a doctor being asked about a recipe: Here's something simple that you can do, sweetie. Tell us how you made these little puff pastries; they're really quite delicious.

Steiner kept his bookish thoughts private; they remained untested in the academy or among learned and literate colleagues. So what did he really know about literature?

He worked in TV; it's what he knew best. He'd spent the last decade of his professional life reviewing young producers' material and saying either "it works" or "it doesn't work." That was his job. Maybe the producers thought he was ruining their work when he changed it, but they rarely said so. Steiner was the boss, after all, and the boss never knows what his employees are truly thinking, just as he never knows if they laugh at his jokes merely because they can see his need to be liked and to amuse.

These days, of course, Steiner had no one to bully, no one who must obey his commands. He knew he'd have another job eventually, despite the woeful economy. There would be new jobs to fill, more contracts to distribute, another small empire to build with somebody else's money. Still, he'd lost his clubhouse, and the small gang of which he'd been the leader. And of course he missed it. He missed walking into a roomful of producers who went silent and were obliged to listen when he talked. He missed being able to help the producers he liked, get them raises and promotions or assignments they coveted. He missed the pleasure of being a provincial monarch. Who wouldn't miss it? Though he downplayed the professional awards his work had won, attributing them to good luck as much as anything else, Steiner soon found himself cherishing the sight of the tacky gold-painted statues as they gathered dust in an open cardboard box in Michael's abandoned bedroom in New York.

"If I'm out of work long enough, I'll have to build an illuminated Lucite box for my Emmys," he told Michael on the phone one night.

"But Dad," his son said, "you don't know how to build anything."

It was after five o'clock in the afternoon when Steiner finally sat down on the bed in Tad and Judith's guestroom to commence his nap. He and Mary had gone out for a walk and a drink at a favorite, pleasantly unchic café with its reassuringly bad lighting and cheap brown vinyl-covered chairs. Some things hadn't changed in Paris.

Steiner read the titles of the books on the shelves that surrounded the bed. Tad and Judith seemed to own five books about every place they'd ever reported on from Bosnia to Hong Kong. This was the book collection of people who needed to quickly gain expertise in a country's culture and history. There were novels, too, mostly recent novels written by journalists, foreign correspondents. The two that Steiner took from the bookcase to sample were signed to Judith by their authors. There were also classics by the more physically adventurous and well-traveled pillars of the Western canon: Kipling, Conrad, Hemingway, Naipaul, and even Melville, who was likely included because of all that sailing around. A few of Mary's titles were mixed in along the shelves. These were gifts from Mary, and Steiner wondered if they'd ever been read. Across from the bed was a framed poster of the cast of a popular TV series. Steiner had never seen the show despite its good press. Odd that Steiner wasn't even curious. He really needed to watch more TV. But it was also odd that Tad had framed the poster. There's no telling the strange things you miss about America when you live abroad.

When Mary opened the heavy wooden bedroom door, she was wearing the quilted white bathrobe Tad and Judith had left for their guests to share. Steiner, surprised to find a warm apartment in this under-heated city, quietly experienced animal happiness. Here was another subject he and Mary were sure to disagree on. Mary, who always yearned for fresh air, liked to sleep with the window open, even in the country house in the dead of winter. For Steiner, this was something his wife did to piss him off, and in her sanctimonious manner Steiner heard his mother-in-law's tiresome Yankee pride. Yet Steiner always had a small crush on his mother-in-law, and she knew it. Catherine was mysterious, bright, willful, and lovely, just like her pain-in-the ass-daughter. You could see why Mary's father, the crazy painter with the Yale degree, had fallen in love with Catherine. But after Mary's father struck Catherine—blackened her eyes—why had he been allowed to return? If Steiner raised his voice to Mary, she seemed to contemplate criminal indictment. Well, times had changed, as had fashions in upper-middle-class domestic disputes. An educated guy just couldn't get away with smacking his wife like in the old days. Even if you professed to be an artist. But then again, poor guys and professional athletes couldn't get away with it anymore, either.

What a crazy old schmuck Mary's father must have been to take his pampered Park Avenue fists to his wife's face. What an uncharacteristic thing for a half-Jewish man to do, Steiner thought, but then again in recent years American Jews really were making great strides in areas where they'd never before really excelled: wife beating, alcoholism, drug abuse, insider trading, corporate crime, and the like.

Mary now opened the French window and turned the handle on the frame of the opposite panel so that the window stayed open a bit. It was a small trick Steiner learned from his Parisian landlady, and he taught it to Mary the first time they came to Paris together.

"The lights just turned on," Mary said.

"Which lights?"

"The Christmas lights," she said, referring to the strings of white lights that—in an impressive display of understated Yuletide elegance—festooned the trees that ran the length of the Boulevard Saint Germain. They really were the perfect set decoration for the beautiful, winding avenue that for decades had haunted Steiner's dreams.

Christmas in Paris, Steiner recalled, was the occasion for relatively restrained municipal and commercial displays and *bûches de Noël* in the windows of all the pastry shops. The rolled cakes were usually pale in color, too, covered with mocha cream icing rather than chocolate.

Parisians liked their Christmas celebrations a bit washed out. France was a Catholic country still, though not a particularly devout one—Catholic with a well-documented atheistic and libertine streak. Which suited Steiner just fine. It was okay to be a little goyish, he liked to tell Mary as she decorated the Christmas trees that she made him drag into their living room each winter—but don't overdo it.

Mary closed the drapes, shutting out that view they both knew they'd miss once they got back to New York to stare at the nice enough post-war reddish brick apartment building that faced them on East 93rd.

Steiner lay on his back, comfortable in the clean sweat pants and cotton T-shirt he'd wear the next morning to go running in the Luxembourg gardens or maybe the Tuilleries if he felt like he could cross the Seine without looking too much like an obsessive American pursuing a ritual utterly lacking in spiritual redemption—though that is surely what he would be.

To Steiner, there was something suspect about how happy he was to be wearing his own soft, clean clothes: it seemed like a shallow form of happiness. On the RER train coming into Paris from the airport, he'd kept falling asleep as they passed through the Queens-like industrial suburban landscape that surrounded the city. But now he wasn't tired, and at this moment, he also felt—what? Sexually excited for some reason: from the stimulation of travel, the conversation with the young French woman, the delicious, slightly chilled Loire Valley red wine he'd had too much of at that café. Or maybe it was the sight of Mary's legs revealed by the half-open white robe when she approached the bed. As soon as she lay down beside him, Steiner decided to dive in.

"No!" Mary shouted, though Steiner couldn't tell for a moment if it was a playful no that meant no or one that meant the opposite. How clean and fresh she tasted. How happy he was to be in Paris. How glad not to still be on that awful plane with its stale air that made Steiner worry he'd catch a cold and get sick even if the damn plane wasn't hijacked and crashed into the Eiffel Tower. Things were going very well so far here in Paris with Mary. Kundera had that line somewhere about it being morally wrong to open your eyes when you kiss. What the hell did that mean? Kundera lived in Paris now, didn't he? Steiner wondered where, in which neighborhood. Such was his interior monologue as he made love with his wife. Or did he make love *to* her? Or were they just having sex? Or screwing? Steiner never knew which phrase he preferred, which he felt was the most honest, but at the moment, he didn't much care as long as events were moving along as planned. Where did Kundera live? Steiner knew Beckett had lived down in the fourteenth arrondissement, near the Prison de Santé. Was that a real prison or an insane asylum? A prison, Steiner thought, because it had guards with guns outside it in those ominous towers along the Boulevard Arago. Balzac lived near there, too, by the Observatoire. Arago was the name of the guy who founded the Observatoire. Steiner decided to head down there for a walk, maybe tomorrow. And that's the neighborhood where he placed Kundera in his imagination. But why is it wrong to keep your eyes open when you kiss your wife? What about when you go down on her? Or when she goes down on you? People really should be careful what they write. Steiner read that line when he was in his twenties, and he took it very much to heart. He'd closed his eyes at intimate moments ever since. Now he was on top of Mary, and he sneaked a peek at his wife just before her climax. Damn Kundera, he's the reason this felt somehow rude, as if Steiner was spying on the person he knew best in the world, the person he loved the most, while they were together doing the most intimate thing two people could do. Mary's eyes were closed. Perhaps she remembered Kundera's line, too. But she seemed to be actually enjoying the familiar humping of the all-too-familiar husband above her, the same one who'd been there doing pretty much the same thing for twenty-three years. Then it ended for Steiner in an impressive fashion, impressive by his standards at least, standards which admittedly had slipped a bit as he grew older and sensations became less vivid, and now Steiner, who could still on a good day read the *Times* without his glasses, thought to himself: Well, I can come about as well as I can see—not so bad but not as good as I used to.

⁎ TWO ⁎

Like the true Parisian driver she'd become, Judith parked her car halfway up on the sidewalk of the Quai de Bourbon on the Île Saint Louis as carelessly as a privileged child leaving a bicycle in front of a country home. Was the car straight? Was it crooked? How many wheels were on the sidewalk? It didn't matter because no one would say anything about it.

"Good enough," Judith said.

"Good enough for Paris," Steiner said from the passenger seat.

"Yes, exactly."

Judith had spent the afternoon negotiating with representatives of Saddam Hussein's government for the right to return to Baghdad. Tomorrow, she'd leave bright and early for what would soon be a war zone. For Judith this was a triumph, but for Steiner it would have been the last thing in the world he wanted to do. He was satisfied to hear Judith's first-hand account from Iraq. There was something prestigious about it: Well, my friend is in Baghdad right now, and she says....

"It's a very cosmopolitan city," Judith told her houseguests in the living room before they all headed out for dinner. "But the Iraqi people are so used to war by now. They've seen so much violence–first the awful war with Iran and then in '91 when we bombed Baghdad. It's a part of normal life for Iraqis. So far there's been no preparation for war or very little. No one is taping up their windows yet. They're trusting their fate to Allah."

"When do you think the war will start?" Mary asked.

"Who knows? February, March. No one knows. But it will come. The American soldiers in Kuwait are all young boys, younger than your son Michael. After I interview them, they almost all ask to borrow my satellite phone. And what do you think are the first words out of their mouth after they dial the phone?"

"What?" Steiner asked.

"'Hi Mom!'" Judith said, imitating the voice of a young man. "They're little boys, so they call their mothers. It breaks your heart."

"My father was nineteen when he fought in the Battle of the Bulge," Steiner said.

"That was terrible, brutal, of course," Judith said. "But this is different. It's the Middle East. It's a huge outdoor weapons bazaar. You'd be surprised how many people there know how to build a bomb."

Judith had arranged for Steiner and Mary to meet two of her colleagues for dinner on the Île Saint Louis—which seemed like an immensely bad idea if eating well was a concern. But at the moment, there might not have been an American in Paris who cared less about food than Steiner: he just wanted to fill his stomach and get back to sleep.

The sight of Notre Dame illuminated by enough light to fill fifty television studios thrilled him. He wondered if Judith or Tad still felt the same way. Steiner silently took in the view of the great cathedral with its illuminated flying buttresses, the only architectural term he remembered from the hours of lectures he'd endured about Gothic cathedrals. For ages people better than him had traveled here from all over the world to take in the very same view. As he followed Judith, Steiner gazed across the Seine towards the Hôtel de Ville, which was lit up in white for the holidays in a way that brought to mind a delicate wedding cake. Once years ago, he and Mary had watched the skaters glide around the small ice rink that was set up in front of the building.

The Île, as Steiner now called it—in imitation of Judith—looked more like an unnaturally preserved precious little village than Steiner remembered. It's all tourist restaurants here, Steiner wanted to say. But why complain? What did it matter? It all comes out your ass the next day, as Steiner once heard a cameraman phrase it when recounting an expensive anniversary dinner with his wife.

Yet could there be a good restaurant on the Île Saint Louis? It seemed impossible. In Balzac's day, perhaps, but not now. It was here on this tiny island in the middle of the Seine that César Birotteau, Balzac's tragic perfume merchant from the Place Vendôme, first saw his future wife, the most beautiful shop girl in all of Paris. Steiner had great affection for all of the innocents on whom Balzac gleefully heaped so much misfortune: sweet, sensitive Cousin Pons, the collector whose chosen heir gets screwed out of a lifetime's worth of accumulated masterpieces; César Birotteau, the naïve entrepreneur who, like Willy Loman, wants only to be well liked, even by the son of a bitch who betrays him. Steiner feared that, like Birotteau, he'd never fully understand the events that were undoing him.

"I'm afraid we're going to talk a little shop," Judith said, as she led her guests across the Quai de Bourbon. So many monarchs were memorialized in this city that was still as cowed by aristocrats as Balzac himself. The great author and the great city shared the same weakness for vanished royalty.

As they approached the restaurant, Judith added a disclaimer. "I've never been to this place, but my friend Jim says he eats there all the time. I hope you like Italian food."

"Italian food our first night in Paris," Mary said in mild protest.

"Sorry," Judith said. "Not my idea."

"Food is the last thing on our minds," Steiner said.

"As long as the wine is good," Mary added.

Which worried Steiner because he somehow doubted that it would be.

"It's not true that you can't get a bad meal in Paris," Steiner said as he held the door open for Judith. "And a bad glass of wine, too. I've proved that you can many times."

It was nine o'clock at night and the restaurant was empty except for the man waving in their direction. This was Jim. The restaurant that nobody but Jim wanted to be in brought to mind those old-fashioned red-sauce Italian joints on Thompson and Sullivan Streets in the Village back in New York. Through the darkness, Steiner saw that a dirty, brownish mural covered the walls. There was the Grand Canal. There was the Bay of Naples.

Jim was certainly a curious sight: longish white hair, blotchy drinker's face. When he stood to kiss Judith on both cheeks, Steiner noticed a dull stain on the lapel of the off-white linen sport coat. Linen in December? Well, only a man who wore linen at Christmas would patronize a deserted Italian restaurant on the Île Saint Louis.

Jim extended his hand for a friendly Midwestern-sounding greeting. The remains of a martini stood in front of him.

"A martini!" Mary said, as warmly as if she'd just seen an old friend or was admiring a particularly cute baby. "I don't think I've ever had a martini in Paris—but it's exactly what I need."

"They make the best martini in Paris here," Jim said.

"Which probably isn't saying much," Judith said.

"No, this is a great martini," Jim said. "I taught the dumb Arab waiter how to make it myself."

He offered Mary a sip from his glass, but she refused, which pleased Steiner. This Jim guy seemed a bit dissipated, and Steiner wouldn't want to share his glass. Something about Jim suggested that he'd survived a few bouts with the clap. It was an irrational image and a libelous accusation, but it came immediately to mind. With his flushed complexion, Jim looked as if half of his person was feverishly engaged in fighting off an exotic infection of some kind.

Jim had lived in Paris "forever," Judith told Steiner and Mary on the way over in the car. He was a stringer for the wire services and production companies from all over the world. He could shoot a story, produce it, even report on camera—whatever was needed. "He used to be quite handsome," Judith said. "And he's good on the air. I saw him live from Baghdad just before the first war. He was one of the last producers they threw out. He has that confidence that works on TV."

Jim now covered everything from fashion shows to strikes and natural disasters all over Western Europe, and he made additional money buying and selling the rights to documentaries: he sold European documentaries to Americans and American documentaries to anyone who wanted them.

"Jim's amazingly well set up," Judith said. "He works when he pleases and enjoys Paris."

If he's so successful, Steiner thought, why is he wearing linen in the winter? Is it the only sport coat the guy owns?

"This place is shit," Jim's friend Buzz said as soon as he joined the party.

"No, it's fine," Jim said. "They know me. I eat here all the time. Have a martini; they're the best in Paris."

"My martini isn't great," Mary said.

"I didn't say it would be great," Jim said. "I said it was the best in Paris."

"You also said it was great," Mary said with the sort of fearless lack of discretion that Steiner himself could only summon in professional situations when he knew he had to speak up to avert a disaster for which he himself might be blamed.

Mary, who already disliked Jim, was getting warmed up to dislike Buzz, though he had not yet even been introduced to the table.

"I'm in Paris for less than a week and this is where you're taking me—for lousy Italian food?" Buzz said to Jim, ignoring everyone else at the table for one more moment. "Well, I'm not paying. This one's on you."

"Fine, fine," Jim said. "Sit down for Christ's sake and act like this isn't the first time you've eaten a meal indoors."

"Buzz Nelson," Jim's friend said, extending his hand first to Judith, who pronounced her own name as she eyed Buzz with the disinterested expression she might also use when meeting a professional bureaucrat whose corruption she planned to soon expose in print.

"We met in Kabul," Judith said. "I'm Tad Wheeler's wife."

"Yes, yes, yes, I remember," Buzz said, though something in his blank gray eyes suggested he never remembered anything.

"For Christ's sake, Buzz, you know Tad," Jim said.

"Of course, I do," he said. Turning to Steiner and Mary he added, "But you two are new, aren't you? We haven't met before."

What was wrong with Steiner, did he instantly hate everybody these days? Did he hate anyone who had a job? Anyone who had an interesting job? Anyone who hadn't worked for him and didn't remember him as a great guy?

"So what do you do?" Buzz asked Steiner.

"TV," Steiner said.

"And what about you?" Buzz said, turning to Mary.

There certainly was an edge to Buzz's tone. Was he the sort of straight guy who hates women or the sort of gay guy who hates women?

Or perhaps he was rude to everybody; it was just his way of showing affection. And what sort of name was Buzz, anyway? But Buzz had certainly chosen the wrong woman to mess with. Mary was almost always offended by indiscreet, direct questions about what she did for a living, especially if they were the first words out of a stranger's mouth.

"I'm a publisher," Mary said.

"And what brings you to Paris?"

"Just visiting," Steiner said.

"So you're tourists," Buzz said.

Okay, he was a tourist: He was a fat, ugly American in white sneakers and a fanny pack waiting in line at the Eiffel Tower and longing for a Big Mac and fries just like he got back home.

"And what brings you to Paris?" Mary asked.

"The Italian food. I hear it's excellent on the Île Saint Louis."

"Buzz is on his way to Qatar and then Baghdad to cover the war," Jim said.

"I'm here to pick up my cameraman and some cash," Buzz said. "I need a lot of cash."

"Who's your cameraman?" Jim asked.

"Abdul."

"Abdul's great," Jim said. "He's fearless."

"He can be a lazy fuck," Buzz said, "like all Arabs. You have to keep after him."

"Arabs aren't lazy," Steiner said quickly. "I refuse to let that pass."

"Most Arabs are lazy," Buzz said. "Most of the ones I've worked with. The ones who were lazy fucks. How many Arabs have you worked with?"

"And the rich Saudis in Paris love whores," Jim said.

"Jim, really," Judith said.

"Buzz, am I telling the truth?"

"Arabs love whores," Buzz said. "You can see them all the time at the Café de la Paix. They get the best whores in Paris."

"You're not suggesting that all Arab men patronize prostitutes, are you?" Mary said, as if she were criticizing a colleague's academic paper.

"I see them backstage at fashion shows chasing all the models," Jim said. "They're very primitive people. What do you think? Do you think they're feminists?"

"I'm just disappointed to hear you talk this way," Judith said. "It's quite ugly."

Steiner was happy to see that the sort of male insults that Jim and Buzz were accustomed to exchanging wouldn't cut it at this table with these particular women. And Buzz might well be one of those tough guys who are afraid of women. Oh, this definitely was the wrong table for Buzz.

"What's all the cash for?" Steiner asked because he was genuinely interested in the logistics of covering a war—as curious as if the job might some day fall into his lap.

"The cash is for bribes," Judith said.

"That's right," Buzz said. "You have to grease palms in the Third World."

Steiner had made Tad explain his job in detail a number of times, but Steiner didn't quite get the nuts and bolts of it: how stories were edited in the field, how the satellite uplinks worked, how an international feed could be broadcast in different languages in different countries. Steiner wondered if he could do the job today if he was plunked down in the middle of Kuwait. It had been years since he'd even cut a feature package himself, and he'd never done a straight news story. How would he proceed in Qatar or Baghdad?

The Arab waiter, a young man of about thirty, came by with the bottle of Fleurie that Jim had chosen, and then asked if the table was ready to order.

"We need a few more minutes," Jim said, in passable French, which he spoke with a defiantly American accent.

Buzz quickly downed his first glass of Fleurie and poured what was left in the bottle into his own glass.

"We need another," Buzz told the waiter in English, shouting across the empty restaurant where the waiter chatted quietly on his cell phone. "More wine. Another bottle."

"Speak French," Jim said.

"Everyone speaks English," Buzz said. "He's an Arab."

No, that's not a toupee that Buzz is wearing, Steiner concluded, but there is something odd about the guy's face which was almost as red as Jim's. He had a pug nose that seemed to have been broken and then

31

stuck back together, and the right side of his face slanted down a bit, as if he might have had a minor stroke. Buzz looked five years older than Steiner, but Steiner guessed they were the same age. Maybe I look this bad and just don't know it, Steiner thought. No, Buzz looked like he'd survived an automobile accident somewhere in the Third World where he'd been quickly patched up by very busy surgeons also tending to more important matters like children pierced with shrapnel.

"What should I order here, darling?" Mary asked because of her belief that Steiner knew more than she did about how to avoid food poisoning in a dump like this.

"Everything's good," Jim said.

"That's why it's so crowded," Mary said.

"Mary!" Judith said with a laugh. "Honestly."

Steiner could not have been more pleased with his wife. It had probably been a while since the last time two smart women made Jim look foolish, and Steiner truly enjoyed the aggrieved look on Jim's face. Welcome to America, pal, he wanted to say. This is what you left behind. This is probably why you left in the first place.

The waiter returned and placed another bottle of Fleurie at the center of the table. The bottle was already open, and Steiner suspected that it might have actually been filled with some sort of cheap generic wine. Buzz immediately filled his glass, and then Jim's.

"I'd like another glass, please," Judith said.

And fuck you, too, Buzz's expression said as he poured the wine.

When Steiner ordered salmon, Mary literally raised an eyebrow. Everyone else seemed to be getting pasta, and Mary chose spaghetti with tomatoes and basil–which seemed to contain nothing that could get spoiled enough to cause acute gastric distress.

"So how much cash are you bringing with you?" Steiner asked Buzz.

"I've got ten grand with me right now, but I don't think it's enough," Buzz said.

"You might be right," Judith told Buzz before turning to Steiner and saying, "Everything costs you over there: your driver, your translator or handler. In Baghdad, everyone has to be paid in cash—American currency."

"I once brought thirty-five grand into Kosovo," Jim said.

32

"Where do you put the money?" Steiner asked.

"In my belt," Buzz said. "It's a money belt. I got it years ago from LL Bean."

"I thought it was illegal to carry that much cash," Steiner said. "Don't they always ask you if you're carrying cash on those forms you have to fill out on the planes?"

"No one tells the truth on those things," Mary said.

It was a long-standing conflict: Steiner preferred to list every purchase he'd made on the customs declaration you were given before landing in New York, while Mary said, "Everyone lies except you, darling." But Steiner always thought, what's wrong with not lying?

"What do you do if they catch you with all that money?" Steiner asked.

"You just say you're a journalist," Judith said.

"They don't care," Buzz said. "Or you bribe them. In the Third World everything is for sale. I went into Afghanistan with twenty grand. The customs guys found it, and they put me in a room. When they saw our equipment, they knew why we had the cash. They knew they couldn't steal it because we had credentials from a major news organization. They just wanted their share. It's a business for them."

"They consider it part of their salary," Jim said.

"You want to see cash?" Buzz said, taking his wallet from his back pocket.

Steiner half expected Buzz to pull out a few grand and lay it in the middle of the table, but instead he produced a folded up piece of foreign currency which he tossed in Steiner's direction.

Showing off, Steiner thought. Buzz is a child who's showing off. Steiner unfolded the bill that had landed in front of him. On it was an engraving of a smiling Saddam Hussein.

"Very nice," Steiner said, holding up the bill for everyone to see.

I remember this, Steiner thought. It's called show and tell.

"Take it," Buzz said. "It's two hundred and fifty Dinars. It's worthless. I once paid a hotel bill with a suitcase filled with those things."

"Thanks," Steiner said, happy to stuff the souvenir into the front pocket of his black jeans.

"Here, take this one, too, Buzz said, throwing another bill Steiner's way. "It's from Afghanistan. Also completely worthless."

Jim had switched from his martini to wine. Mary's half-full martini glass stood in front of her.

"Afghanistan is where you got fucked up, isn't it?" Jim asked Buzz.

"It wasn't that bad."

"What happened?" Judith asked.

Journalists certainly are direct, Steiner could not help but notice. Well, it was a good way to get the facts.

"Nothing," Buzz said, pouring himself more wine.

"What do you mean nothing? You got blown up," Jim said, reaching in front of Judith for more wine.

Oh, that's why Buzz's face looks fucked up, Steiner realized, because it *is* fucked up. Buzz was literally fucked up by history–no kidding around. His nose didn't seem to have any cartilage, his face sagged, and he was a drunk. And he kept putting himself in harm's way. Buzz was clearly committing a slow suicide—not unlike the rest of us, Steiner thought.

"It was an accident," Buzz said. "It's nothing."

"I don't know," Jim told his friend. "You look like shit."

"So do you, my friend," Buzz told Jim.

"What happened?" Judith asked, more or less demanding details.

"A mortar went off halfway across the field in Afghanistan. It was at the end of the war. I wasn't really near it when it went off. I was out for a while. But I was fine. They wanted to evacuate me to Germany, but I wouldn't let them."

"And you keep going back?" Mary asked.

"It's what I do," Buzz said.

Perhaps Steiner had never covered a war and didn't know that wealthy Arabs hung out with their whores at the Café de la Paix, but he had produced a child while these guys probably slept with whores themselves. There was no doubt that Jim and Buzz were working with very interesting material. They had enviable careers. Yet this by itself did not make them interesting men. If something fascinating happens to a dull person, that person is still dull, though anecdotes can camouflage their pedestrian minds. People with first-rate intellects rarely have first-rate adventures, Steiner told himself. This is the category of contemporary middle-class Americans he secretly put himself in.

As soon as Steiner's salmon was placed in front of him, he doubted that he'd be able to eat it. It was the sort of bad-smelling fish that—when it passed by their table at a restaurant—always prompted Mary to say, "I'm glad I didn't order *that*."

Mary, looking up grimly from her sad-looking pasta, flared a nostril and asked, "How's your fish?"

"Haven't tasted it yet," Steiner said.

"My pasta's delicious," Jim said.

Steiner took a bite: it didn't taste like salmon. It didn't taste like fish. What did it taste like? He didn't care. Steiner spit his food out into his napkin.

"I can't eat that," he said.

"What's wrong?" Jim asked.

"It smells awful," Mary said.

"Do you want to taste it?" Steiner asked her.

"I don't have to. I can smell it from here."

"Listen," Steiner told Jim, "I'll send it back, but my French is a little shaky, so you'll have to back me up."

"Don't worry," Jim said, and he actually winked at Steiner. "I'll handle it."

"Waiter!" Buzz shouted in English. "We've got some bad fish here."

The waiter ended his cell phone conversation and walked wearily across the room. Steiner surprised himself by lowering his voice a few octaves—as he often did when speaking French—and returning the fish with the self-righteous poise of a card-carrying member of the bourgeoisie. Who was this person telling the waiter in a deep voice, *"Je vous assure monsieur, je ne peut pas le manger."* It was Steiner, who felt strangely unconnected to his own French voice. It's fun to be someone else, Steiner thought, especially if you're usually me.

The debate lasted a couple of minutes until the waiter finally took back the fish and agreed to bring a salad Niçoise, plus the additional bottle of wine that Buzz asked for before he merrily reminded the table, "Jim's paying for me, so I might as well get drunk."

35

Through it all, Jim remained as silent as a school kid who had done something wrong and was content to say nothing while one of his friends caught all the blame.

"Hey Jim," Steiner said, "thanks for watching my back."

⸱ THREE ⸱

Steiner was surprised to see the sun in the middle of a December morning in Paris. In his memory of this city from November through March, it rained every day. Make that every day from October to May. But Steiner guessed it was now close to fifty degrees, and oddly enough, he didn't see a single cloud in the sky that he always thought of as gray but somehow luminous, too. Standing just outside Tad and Judith's place and watching the traffic on the familiar Boulevard Saint Germain, he was happy to be where he was. Mary had gone out first, and they were to meet in fifteen minutes for their morning coffee. The feel of the soft chill air on Steiner's face was entirely pleasant, as was the dull and steady roar of the Citroëns, Peugeots, and Mercedes. Tad and Judith really were well set-up. Tad even had his car shipped over from the States, and he drove it around Paris with New York license plates. That Tad was able to navigate those plates through the massive bureaucracy that governed this country was a testament to his impressive mastery of all things French. And all Tad and Judith needed to do was risk their lives regularly reporting the news from the very scary places. By now Judith was in the air on the way to Baghdad; Steiner had heard the door slam when she left at five in the morning. Well, she and Tad certainly deserved a great apartment, even if they were rarely around to enjoy it.

To the east was the familiar, reddish façade of the Brasserie Lipp with its small glassed-in terrace. "No salad served as main course," it famously said in English on the bottom of the menu posted in front of the restaurant—which always made Steiner want to go in and order a salad as his main course, just for the fun of observing the predictable outrage.

Now Steiner saw his wife. There was Mary, directly across the grand boulevard. There was the defiant stride he loved so much. Was it possible that her gait was intelligent? It was certainly deliberate. Mary paused in front of the Sonia Rykiel women's boutique and inspected the window display with the sort of seriousness that she focused on paintings at the Metropolitan Museum of Art. Well, her father had taught her how to see a painting, understand the issues involved from an artist's perspective. "Open your eyes," she'd tell Michael in a museum. "Tell me what you see." Steiner was sure Mary's old man had used the same exact words on his precocious daughter countless times.

Steiner hurried across the street, and stood maybe ten feet away from Mary but she didn't see him. So *that's* what she was looking at. The store's Christmas windows featured Pléiade editions of great French writers: Hugo, Zola, Baudelaire, Rimbaud, Proust. A larger-than-life, stern photo of one esteemed author dominated the center of each window, and the stately Pléiade volumes with their burgundy and gold-striped bindings lined the bottom of the displays.

Steiner briefly and guiltily enjoyed the feeling of spying on his wife before taking a few steps forward until he was close enough to bark out a deep-voiced, "Bonjour."

Mary turned with her fiercest New York "fuck you" expression, and Steiner could do nothing but grin: he was very glad to see her, and at the moment he loved even her outraged anger. Mary returned the smile, laughing at her own severity, and the two said nothing for a moment, and then another moment. They just looked at each other in silence, delighted to find themselves in Paris together. Well, why not? So few things made them happy these days, they both realized, even though they knew this was their own stupid fault.

Finally, they kissed.

"Where's Honoré?" Steiner asked.

"I'm not sure he made the cut."

Balzac, it turned out, hadn't been awarded a place of honor on the boulevard. His portrait faced a side street, rue des Saint Pères. Yet another disappointment for the genius who was never elected to the Académie Français. Well, Honoré would survive.

One non-literary figure, the fashion designer Karl Lagerfeld, had been given his own window by the main entrance of the store. Lagerfeld's new diet book was on view along with all those literary masterpieces. A joke, no doubt, and not a bad one, in Steiner's view. From leafing through Mary's copies of *Vogue*, Steiner knew that Lagerfeld, a German, worked for either Chanel or Dior, one of those old French houses. But the Lagerfeld Steiner remembered was a bloated Buddha-like figure who always carried a fan. He was nothing like the emaciated figure in the photo in the window.

"My God," Steiner said. "The guy must have lost a hundred pounds."

Though this was not the sort of psychological transformation that Mary valued so much in her Jungian way, Lagerfeld had remade his physical self, which was impressive.

"He looks great," Mary said. "He deserves to have his diet book face the Boulevard Saint Germain. I wonder if he has an American publisher."

"Does Lagerfeld design Chanel or Dior?" Steiner asked.

"Chanel, of course," Mary said, with the sort of fan's knowledge that Michael displayed when discussing his favorite musical groups—the ones that interested Steiner not one bit. "And he does Fendi too, I think. He used to design Chloé, but no more."

"What happened at Chloé? Was he fired?"

"I'm not sure," Mary told her husband, as she took his hand. "But he's not there anymore. You know what that's like, don't you darling?"

Yes, he certainly did.

* * *

The firings—layoffs really—had been brutal, as all such events must be. Through a friend at company headquarters in far-off New Jersey, Steiner learned ahead of time that drastic cuts were coming, and that all the executives at his level in the New York office would lose their jobs, along with sixty percent of the staff. It was not a surprise. The stock of the parent company had dropped over eighty percent after the Internet bubble burst. By the time the layoffs came, almost everybody—from producers to production assistants—knew they were imminent. Steiner had seen it coming from the moment he was hired. A job like his was like managing a Major League baseball team—sooner or later your ass gets fired. He made TV shows. The ratio of success to failure in the business was equal to the odds against winning at a Vegas casino. The layoffs made sense to Steiner, and he told Mary, "This is the first logical thing the company's done since I got there."

Steiner had begun his stint in corporate life boasting that he knew nothing about business, though it was not altogether true. He understood how to manage a budget for a television show—to plan to spend millions of dollars and come in on budget at the end of the year or the run of the show. It was as simple as balancing your checkbook. What was new and somewhat baffling at first were meetings filled with talk of five-year plans, returns on investment, corporate takeovers, shareholder value, and the like. Still, the company's grandiose expansion plans seemed illogical, though Steiner assumed his reservations were due to his ignorance of how capitalism worked.

When he was hired during the late 1990s, the stock of the parent company was approaching an all-time high and the corporation was lousy with cash. Several of the people Steiner worked with were millionaires thanks to their stock options. His colleagues' wealth did not make them smart, but it made them jolly. And it was almost impossible for them to think that they did not deserve the money. Their wealth felt like the manifestation of justice that had been delayed for too long. Finally, the world agreed with what they secretly thought about themselves: they were very special after all. Steiner particularly cherished a line from *The Rise and Fall of Cèsar Birotteau* in which Balzac writes that the merchant Birotteau mistook the summit of his career for the starting-point. Steiner realized that he, too, had succumbed to the syndrome. Well, there had been something seductive about the tacit agreement he made fortnightly in return for the paycheck that was automatically deposited into his bank account; his annual thirty-percent bonus; and the stock options he'd come to expect each spring. Steiner thought of these three forms of payments as carrots dangled in front of him while he circled a racetrack. Yet unlike a racehorse, Steiner got to eat the carrots. And it sometimes seemed that the corporation had calculated the precise size of the carrot needed to make Steiner run as fast as he could and still feel that he was receiving sufficient reward for his exertions.

So Steiner adhered to his unspoken agreement with the company: he put in the hours, even at the expense of domestic happiness; he voiced his opinion, but if his advice was ignored, he accepted the decided-upon plan and implemented it as best he could; if a plan changed or failed, he didn't point out the ironies, and he never reminded anybody that they had been wrong.

Steiner wasn't sure that those were the precise rules his bosses would articulate if pressed, but he stuck to them nonetheless. Twice a month, when Steiner opened his pay stub—or when he deposited his bonus or cashed in a few stock options—Steiner was as happy as a child on Christmas morning, though his pleasure was deeper because he knew how rare the gifts were and how easily they could stop because they came from people who really didn't give a shit about him.

When the value of the company's stock began to fall, Steiner met with his broker to discuss cashing in all his remaining stock options. They were still worth over half a million dollars. Why not take the bird in the hand? Waving a forecast by an analyst so well publicized that even Steiner knew her name, the broker predicted that the stock would rebound and go even higher.

"But what the company is doing makes no sense to me," Steiner said.

"Everyone thinks their own company is stupid," came the reply.

The broker was a charming bully, which is to say Steiner allowed himself to be charmed. By a salesman! He let himself be charmed by a salesman who happened to have gone to his college five years after Steiner graduated. They'd had the same teacher for freshman composition. As if that gave them something in common. And the broker was literate, so Steiner was cowed. All it took was a couple of lines from Yeats or Auden—and even Frank O'Hara—and Steiner was sold. The broker had noticed that Steiner had a weakness for poetry, like some men have a weakness for a free steak dinner in a pricey midtown restaurant.

Steiner sold a fraction of the options, and watched passively as the others became as worthless as Confederate dollars. Each morning, after he squinted to check the stock's value in the paper, he did nothing. Morning after morning. Nothing but uncomprehending passivity and blindness.

How could he have not seen what was happening to the stock when it was so clear? Perhaps it was too subtle: the stock dropped two points one week, then three points the next. No, it was denial. The ineluctable facts didn't register. Steiner was like the fat person in the doctor's office insisting that the scale is inaccurate. When Steiner read about this sort of personal financial disaster in Balzac, he'd think: How could the characters be so blind? Don't they know they're in a Balzac novel where the naïve and greedy always lose out? Only later did Steiner realize that he was a character in his own personal Balzac novel, not a reader.

During the Christmas break following 9/11, Michael confessed to his parents that he found himself fantasizing about moving back in time.

"Like it's a week before 9/11," he told Steiner and Mary over dinner at their favorite East Side bar. Michael did not confide in them often anymore, but his imagination was bothering him. "So what would I do?" the boy continued. "I know there's going to be an attack and I'm the only American who knows what's going to happen because I've traveled backward in time. But I'm just a freshman in college—just one person. So I go to the FBI or *The New York Times* or something and I make up a story: I was in a taxi and the cab driver told me everything—the names of the leaders, where their planes took off, the whole thing. But I tell the FBI that when I looked for the driver's hack license, it wasn't where it normally is. And then when I tried to see his face, it was covered with a beard, a hat, and sunglasses. And I say that he made me swear I wouldn't say anything else about him. He just wanted me to warn the authorities."

Months later, Steiner found himself having a fantasy of his own: he imagined moving backward in time and cashing in his stock options. He fantasized about telling his broker to sell it all despite the expert advice. Like his son, Steiner found that his unconscious mind reran its hackneyed plot over and over again, defying his efforts to change the channel.

Once Steiner's chance to make a small killing had vanished, he took away a lesson: his ability to understand narrative was his only protection against the hugely inventive and seductive sophistries of American capitalism.

Business plans were predictions, but Steiner came to think of them as fictions. Though he had no training in business, he'd read a lot of novels, and he understood when a story was logical. When a business plan seemed not to cohere, it was probably not the fault of Steiner's inability to fully grasp the mysteries of commerce. It was more likely that the narrative didn't make sense, the plan was flawed, people were lying to themselves. But then again, Steiner sometimes suspected that he had not been privy to all the relevant information—that the corporation's highest motivations were kept secret.

The company he worked for was a luxury yacht, Steiner always told Michael as they rowed their tiny dinghy around the deep harbor near their summer home. When the yachts passed by, the rowboat rocked in their wake, though the owners of the huge vessels weren't aware of the turbulence they'd left behind. Nor did they likely care. The analogy was obvious, and Michael had heard it so many times that late one afternoon last summer, he told his father, "Maybe you should get yourself a bigger boat, Dad."

With rumors of the coming layoffs spreading through the office, Steiner took a company car out to New Jersey to chase down his boss, Bill Fuller. The drive through New Jersey to the "mother ship," as the main building of the company's headquarters was known, made Steiner feel as numb as he did while changing planes in any airport hub in America: he felt like he was nowhere because everything that surrounded him—from the uniforms of the airline employees to the stores and fast food joints—was generic. These New Jersey highways, these low-slung office buildings with their tinted windows, the gas stations, the franchise restaurants—these were the places Steiner, a very predictable Manhattan snob, had labored his whole life to avoid.

A year before he was laid off, Steiner confided to his assistant, "I give myself six months at most." Though the job lasted longer than he expected, it was odd to predict that something would happen, half *want* it to happen, but half hope somehow to be saved. He had enemies, sure. But that just meant he was properly defending his small piece of corporate turf. And Steiner had mastered the art of patronizing the budget-watchers and personnel powerhouses who constituted his company's deeply suburban, resentful permanent bureaucracy. He found a way to work with them all, a way to like something within each one of them and make them like him, too, he hoped. In the end, he could have tried to talk his way into saving his job. He watched a colleague do it rather shamelessly, or cravenly, really, and Steiner even knew who he'd talk to in the company and what he'd say. But he had too much pride.

As he showed his corporate ID to the sleepy security guard in New Jersey that day, and then walked noiselessly on carpeted floors among plump-faced executives to the silent elevator at headquarters, Steiner just wanted to go back home. Yet there were times, after he'd been laid off, when all he wanted was to again be in some woeful meeting at that very same overly air-conditioned building, sneaking a peek at his watch as he looked forward to sharing a bottle of red wine with Mary in their Manhattan apartment with its habitable temperature and wooden floors which, after a few hours in the suburbs, seemed like the embodiment of everything that he loved about the civilized world.

"So does this mean I'm losing my job?" Steiner asked Bill Fuller as soon as they sat face-to-face in Bill's office with its suburban expanse of unused space. Steiner of course already knew the answer to his question.

"Probably yes," Bill said, by which he meant absolutely yes.

It was an awful moment, awful because Steiner wanted the man he didn't respect to say something kind to him, and Bill didn't possess the instinct to say it: he had no gift for patronizing his employees. Bill may have been the least forthcoming man Steiner had ever known; he totally lacked an autobiographical impulse. He was guarded in the way that people are when they have something to hide—a scandal or their own incompetence.

Bill was universally thought to be attractive, and it would have pleased Steiner to observe that Bill's good looks were somehow compromised by failure of character, but it wasn't the truth. When Bill spoke, people felt better. When he smiled, you liked him; and when he offered praise, it felt as if not a father, but perhaps a wealthy older brother, had patted you on the back. Bill's dark suits were sophisticated and modern, but not so chic as to offend provincial sensibilities. He swam every morning before work, so he was quite fit. And it was impossible to judge his ethnicity by his physical appearance. His dark complexion could have made him part Italian or Spanish, but that straight-ahead manner and Eastern accent were pure Yankee. At the company Christmas party two years back, Steiner matter-of-factly asked Bill's secretary to solve the mystery of his ethnic origin. "Bill's an American," the young girl said. Well, that didn't help much.

"You'll be taken care of," Bill told Steiner across the desk that Bill kept free of clutter, a habit intended, Steiner thought, to bespeak clarity and power, to imply that the man who worked here was not fully of this world, but focused instead on lofty corporate strategy. Yet the empty desk seemed to Steiner like a metaphor for Bill's empty mind and empty heart. When Bill said, "taken care of," Steiner remembered that his father had used these words when talking about the attendants in the men's locker room at the country club. Each Christmas, they were taken care of, meaning that Murray Steiner handed them a tip in defiance of club rules. But Steiner understood that his cooperation was being purchased with a severance package, and he was glad for it. Given the circumstances, silence was all that Steiner had to sell.

A week later, one hundred and twenty-six people gathered in the studio that Steiner had helped design. The set for one of his shows was up, so the frightened group was surrounded by hundreds of thousands of dollars worth of scenery as they waited to be told their fate. The set had cost more than Steiner spent seven years earlier on his summer house. Soon the flats would be trashed, he knew, and placed in bins to be hauled away.

Steiner gave Bill Fuller a dutiful smile. This was the somber grin Steiner used at funerals. It was meant to tell Bill that Steiner was not taking the coming professional catastrophe personally. Because no one in corporate life is supposed to take anything personally, even though what happens is often very personal indeed. At the moment, Steiner believed that if the company ever told Bill Fuller that he should beat Steiner to a pulp using a baseball bat, Bill might go home, take a good look at his wife and kids, remember how much he loved them and how much he loved his money, and report to work the next day with bat in hand.

Following the plan that Steiner had been briefed on earlier that morning, Bill, who'd been fitted with a wireless microphone, quickly confirmed that there would be layoffs. He then did what Steiner had suggested: he commended everyone on their hard work and the quality of the programming they'd produced. The producers seemed to take the praise to heart, even the more cynical older ones who'd been through something like this many times. Who wouldn't want to hear a kind word from a surrogate father even as he was tossing you out of the house?

Bill's voice began to quiver, and then he choked up. There was something nicely comical about the way the tears came into Bill's eyes. He didn't want to cry, but the flow erupted. His chest convulsed slightly, as if he'd swallowed spoiled milk.

Disdain registered on the face of the smart young producer beside Steiner. She'd always been one of his favorites.

"He's crying for himself," she whispered, leaning in close.

Steiner now experienced a small erotic frisson at being so physically near this talented woman, though he'd previously spent hours in dark editing rooms sitting just inches away from her without feeling the slightest sexual pull. Steiner tried not to smile.

Bill pulled out his prop: a typed list of names. "It's the way they always do it," Bill had explained to Steiner. "We have to follow the formula."

Without making eye contact with all the anxious people before him, Bill told the group, "A copy of this list will be distributed to you. Those of you whose names are on the list should report to the conference rooms next to your name. The rest of you, please go back to your desks."

All assembled knew immediately that the people on the list had lost their jobs. Steiner knew that there would not be a room assignment after his name. His severance package was to be discussed in the privacy of his office, and Steiner was anxious about the degree to which he'd be taken care of.

After telling his favorite producers, "That's show business; TV jobs always end," Steiner stopped into the men's room down the hall from the control room where he was no longer the boss. While Steiner stood at the urinal, a man vomited in one of the stalls. One spasm of retching. Silence. Then another brief spasm. As Steiner washed his hands, Bill Fuller emerged unembarrassed from the stall, wiping his mouth with his hand.

"It never gets any easier," Bill said. His tanned forehead was beaded with cold sweat.

Steiner, contemplating his own surprisingly merry expression in the mirror, said nothing.

After gargling with tap water and subjecting his handsome face to a vigorous rinsing off, Bill said, "That was very hard for me to do."

"I've found," Steiner said, "that situations such as this are usually worse for the people being fired than the people doing the firing."

Later that day, Steiner turned in his corporate ID, his company laptop and cell phone, the key to the office, the key to the studio, and the electronic pass that allowed him to buzz into the midtown office building where security had been unrelentingly tight since 9/11.

"Do you want my gun and my badge?" Steiner asked the Human Resources representative he'd done business with for the past five years. Rosemarie was a heavyset woman who was raising three daughters in New Jersey with her husband, who also worked in HR for the company. Steiner could usually make her laugh, but she didn't laugh this time. She used a rubber band from a box on her desk to bind together the artifacts of his time with the company for inventory later on. As Steiner headed back to his office to change the outgoing message on his answering machine, he remembered that Rosemarie's brother was a cop who'd been paralyzed from the waist down after he was shot years ago. What an idiot I am, Steiner thought, and he went back immediately to apologize.

"It's been a tough day all around," Rosemarie said.

They'd been through plenty together. Rosemarie did Steiner's paperwork when he was hired; he'd fought with her and won over hiring a kid who'd failed to appear for her mandatory drug screening test; but she'd helped Steiner when he wanted to get raises for his hardest-working employees. They took pleasure in conspiring to push the increases through the formidable bureaucracy without breaking any of its complex rules. If they'd gone to the same high school, they would never have been friends, but she taught Steiner how to work the system she'd spent her adult life in, and they'd found a way to like and respect one another. Steiner held out his arms and gave her a hug.

"I'm sorry," he said.

"I didn't think you liked hugs," Rosemarie said as they separated. "I'm sorry you got canned."

"Not as sorry as I am," Steiner said.

He knew they'd never see each other again.

As Steiner left the office for the last time towards six o'clock that night, he said good-bye to a group of production assistants and editors who stood gossiping in the hallway as he passed. They were among those who had not lost their jobs, and they were doubtless experiencing what the psychologists call survivor's guilt. The kids spontaneously broke into applause, praise for Steiner's work, he thought.

"Thank you," he told them simply, placing his left hand over his heart. "Thank you so much."

Where the hell did that gesture came from? Steiner didn't know: it surprised him, but he was not embarrassed by it. There were worse things in life than being sincere. When he was alone in the elevator, there were tears in his eyes.

As Steiner told Mary the story that night over a glass of Bordeaux, little tears appeared in her eyes, too. Steiner felt a mighty sense of relief. At that moment, she might have chosen to remind her husband about how blind and arrogant he'd been; how he'd expected the money to never stop flowing; how he'd allowed the corporation to silently fill the spaces in his heart where deeper, truer feelings belonged. All of that was true enough.

"You were crying because somebody who worked for you actually noticed that you did a good job," Mary said.

"I wasn't actually crying," Steiner said. "I just teared up."

"Your feelings are hurt, darling," Mary said. "And they should be."

Steiner hadn't thought of it that way, but surely Mary was right: his feelings *were* hurt. Why not admit it? And there was the money, too. He would miss the money. So would Mary. Still, the family had no real immediate worries. Despite Steiner's poor judgment on the stock options, he had what felt like a small fortune in savings. If the stock market hadn't tanked, he'd have had even more. Then there was Mary's money, stashed away in various conservatively managed accounts. Steiner wasn't sure exactly how much it came to, but he guessed his wife had at least as much money as he did: after all, they lived off his salary, and hers was slated for use during their fast-approaching old age. And the money they'd prudently, boringly—and at Mary's insistence— saved for Michael's college tuition was in a separate bank account waiting to be spent. Steiner's savings didn't amount to all that much by the standards of his friends with apartments on Park Avenue or high above lower Manhattan. But by the standards of most of the world, he was rich enough. In New York, of course, he was at best comfortably middle class. Still, Steiner was as proud of his financial assets as any of Balzac's great misers. When he balanced his checkbook on Saturday mornings, Mary teased him by calling him "Gobseck," Balzac's ubiquitous moneylender. That Gobseck was one of Balzac's anti-Semitic caricatures seemed not to trouble his twenty-five percent Jewish wife— which troubled Steiner, though not all that much.

* * *

"*Et voilà!*" the elaborately polite, talkative, middle-aged woman behind the counter at the Louvre of a sock department in Bon Marché said as she handed Steiner a delicate blue crinkly paper bag containing three pairs of the English-made, knee-length Argyle socks Steiner bought every time he came to Paris. For some reason, the socks were not available anywhere in New York.

As was their habit when on vacation together in Paris, Mary and Steiner had separated at mid-morning. They'd meet up again for drinks and tell each other what they'd done. In New York, they never spent their whole day together, so why do it here? After he kissed Mary goodbye following breakfast at a café near the Sonia Rykiel boutique, Steiner walked aimlessly to the east in the general direction of the Boulevard Raspail.

When he was a student living alone a few blocks from where he now found himself, Steiner often would choose a neighborhood he didn't know well, read through the clunky prose of his *Blue Guide*, travel to the strange neighborhood via the Metro, get lost, consult his *Indispensable* to figure out where he was, and then walk home, usually getting lost once or twice along the way. The self-guided tours took hours, long enough to occupy the bulk of a Saturday or Sunday. In those days, Steiner treated the whole ancient, exquisitely lit city like one large museum, as he passed through Les Halles, the Marais, Clichy, Montparnasse, Passy, and all the rest. He looked at landmarks, ordinary buildings, stores, and people, but didn't speak to anyone except the shopkeepers and café waiters he could not avoid.

Even today, Steiner, who otherwise never rode a subway or train— or sat in a waiting room, bar or any place else—without reading his *Times* or his Balzac, could entertain himself at any out-of-the way café simply by watching Parisians go about their business. Besides the predictable pleasure of eyeing the attractive women, Steiner studied the way Parisians rushed for the bus in the rain, walked their dogs, tied their scarves, ordered their drinks, greeted each other with double kisses—or those oddly hurried but deliberate handshakes.

Being in Paris, where Steiner was not known, was something of a relief: it was a city that did not frown upon those who idled away the day. It was a good place to be out of a job. Yet Steiner was embarrassed to have no real reason to be in Paris, just as he was embarrassed that there was at present nothing he was obliged to do anywhere in the world.

And what *would* he be doing in Paris, he wondered, as he approached the most formidable-looking hotel in the sixth, the Lutétia, where one of Mary's authors, a South African, had been put up by the French government when they flew him to Paris to get the Legion of Honor. Something to do with the Holocaust had taken place at the Lutétia, Steiner knew. The buildings of Paris were footnoted with the precision of a scholarly text, so there was a plaque on the side of the building that told the story. But Steiner was not inclined to cross the street. Had the Lutétia been the Nazi headquarters? No, that was the Meurice on the rue de Rivoli. The old photos of the Nazi flag hanging outside the stately hotel still held a brutal power: they made Steiner feel like Hamlet contemplating the sight of his mother in the arms of his father's brother and murderer. Yes, the Nazis had really been here a mere decade before Steiner was born. The Allies shot it out with the Germans in the lobby of the Meurice, and shots had been fired in the Luxembourg Gardens. Though Steiner had heard that you could still see the bullet holes in the fence that surrounded the Gardens, he had never been able to find them for himself. Well, he might take another look today: it wasn't like he had anything else to do.

As anyone might have predicted, a pigeon sat indifferently on the head of Rodin's bronze monument to Balzac near the Vavin Metro stop. No one seemed to be paying Honoré much mind except for a Japanese couple who looked back and forth from their guidebook to the sculpture. To Steiner, the monument seemed smaller than he remembered. He had read that Balzac was supposed to be touching his own phallus beneath his great cloak, and Rodin had certainly situated Honoré's hands in the appropriate place if this was true. It did look a bit as if the great author was playing with himself. But Steiner wasn't sure he believed it. What was the point? Most great artists could be accused of playing with themselves in one way or another, but the result was work that was of universal interest. Was Balzac guiltier of self-involvement than other geniuses? Why would Rodin be so outrageously rude?

It wasn't yet noon, and Steiner had already achieved everything he'd set out to do that day: he'd bought the socks and seen the statue. Not much to be proud of there.

At Steiner's age, the most dignified way to visit a city was to work there, to be on assignment with someone else picking up the bill for the seat in business class, the oversized room, the taxis, and the meals. To be immensely busy was to be alive and respected in the modern world. If you were working in LA, Paris, London—or even the battlefields where Tad and Judith flourished—you were experiencing a place through the eyes of a professional. Here in Paris, as Buzz had pointed out, Steiner was a mere tourist, which made him feel like one of the American provincials he saw in Times Square attempting to figure out which way was uptown. Almost everyone was at some time a tourist, yet of all the creatures on earth, few were as looked-down upon as tourists were. Had Steiner not lost his job, these thoughts would not be afflicting him. But the anxieties arrived nonetheless like a cold that arrived—like all colds do—at exactly the wrong time.

Well, one thing Steiner was going to do in Paris was more shopping, he realized, as he headed north on the always popular, narrow, winding rue du Cherche Midi. No wonder everyone loved this street with its

51

delicate little buildings: it was suffused with light and—most importantly of all perhaps—filled with small boutiques.

As Steiner turned onto the rue de Grenelle, shopping here in Paris felt like a socially acceptable, even masculine distraction. "In a year you won't look back and think, 'I'm sorry I spent so much money on that great-looking jacket,'" Mary told Steiner that morning before they separated. The words comforted him as he eyed pricey shoes through windows, strolled into stores, fingered sweaters, tried on sport coats, and attempted to dodge the hard sell of the French shop clerks. This was Steiner's way of engaging the culture, gathering information. A few hours looking over the beautifully made clothing before making perhaps one purchase was something of an aesthetic experience—a lazy, less-demanding, narcissistic version of time at a museum.

The slim young woman who now faced him across the counter was absurdly pretty in a fragile way. Tight little black sweater, short red skirt, black tights, and of course, heels. Straight white teeth, a bit too much mascara for Steiner's taste, not unintelligent pale green eyes: she was sort of a younger French version of Mary. The woman had dyed her hair a bright, artificial red, but the effect was playful and attractive: she was having fun with her own beauty rather than protesting against it like an angry punk from years ago. It really was a pleasure to look at her; she was her own small masterpiece.

And what luck to have stumbled upon the only salesperson left in the sixth arrondissement who spoke no English. As Steiner acquired yet another black pullover, he enjoyed chatting with this otherworldly creature who was obliged to answer his questions, pretend to be amused by his small jokes, and tolerate his unsteady French. Yes, he was from New York, he told her. No, she had never been there. Yes, he visited Paris often. No, she did not think the sweater was too small on Steiner: he had a nice form, and that is how it was intended to be worn. How many times a day was this woman obliged to tolerate the flirtatious talk of a barely bi-lingual, middle-aged American man purchasing an overpriced *pull*?

It was all vanity, unrequited narcissism. But Steiner had worked hard to earn his money, and this was how he chose to spend it. Having read his Balzac, he understood that money became more important as you got older: it cushioned you from the world. It was a balm that eased the pain of what Mary called the encroaching smallness of their lives, by which she meant the life that lay before them as a couple whose son had finally left home; the prospect of evenings staring at each other across the dinner table and weekends of doing and saying what they always did and said.

"*Merci, Monsieur*," the salesgirl seemed to sing as she handed Steiner the exquisitely wrapped sweater. Perhaps she was just buoyed by the prospect of Steiner finally leaving the store. The cliché was true: nowhere in the world were they more gifted at putting things in tissue paper and bags, Steiner thought, though he could scarcely claim to have seen the world at all. Yet Steiner was satisfied with his transaction in a way that he would not have permitted himself to be in New York City if he'd accomplished nothing more than buy a turtleneck in an empty store before lunch time.

The return to a more innocent self was likely why Steiner dragged his ass over here so often. It was a bit like cheating on your wife with a younger woman without the burdens of deception or the pleasures of young flesh. One reason men abandoned their wives was the fun of retelling old stories to someone who would be easily impressed, would laugh in all the right places. Suddenly, all the used-up material became new again, and a man could feel like a performing artist re-emerging from decades of obscurity to a fresh, slightly naïve audience that was easily impressed by the old hits. The very stories whose charms your wife had grown immune to now entertained the young girl at your side. It was like discovering the stock you thought was worthless had regained its value.

⚓ FOUR ⚓

"This feels just like New York," Steiner said as he and Mary rode the number four Metro line north past Châtelet, past the Gare du Nord, and up towards Montmartre where their friends Johnny and Claire lived with their five children. Steiner meant that the Metro car, with its New York-like mix of ethnicities, seemed familiar. He was surrounded by as many black people and Arabs as white people. Perhaps more. While the center of Paris often seemed like a theme park in which one of the themes was privileged white people being white together, this part of the city felt more like home.

Steiner tried to eavesdrop on the slangy, fast-paced dialogue between the two teenage girls holding onto the pole above him. But he couldn't quite get what they were saying—which reminded him of the first time he sat in the control room of a TV studio watching the director shout cryptic instructions to the technical director, the assistant director, the cameramen, the stage manager, the tape operator, and all the others whose jobs Steiner didn't yet understand.

But what did Steiner really know about the French? Because he didn't speak the language fluently, Steiner's contact with this society was filtered through a veil. So being in Paris was like his ordinary, alienated experience of the modern world, but more so. It was even more alienating because during almost every encounter with a Frenchman, Steiner was reminded of his inability to fully understand what was happening. Was it possible to be a failed Francophile?

Steiner held the editorial page of the *Herald Tribune*; Mary inspected the rest of the paper with her skeptical professional editor's expression. Mary read a newspaper the way Steiner watched TV, in the rare instances when he did watch TV: with a disinterested air reflecting equal amounts of collegial understanding and jealousy.

For Mary, Steiner's devotion to the *Times* or the *Tribune* was a suspect addiction, a way of dulling the complexities of life with a well-written, highly rational narcotic. These newspapers gave Steiner the illusion that he understood the world, that it was more ordered than it really was. But now that Steiner had nothing but time, the pages of his morning paper had turned to ash. Now that he had the time to read every word of the paper, he didn't want to. Certain stories he still followed—stories about politics, the TV business, and, of course, stories about terrorists, the people who had blown up a piece of his city and would surely try to do it again because they said they would and the thing about those motherfuckers was they always kept their psychotic word.

"Oh my God," Mary said, pointing at the paper. "Look at this."

There was Philip on page three. There was Mary's ex-husband, her first husband. Philip had been an actor, which is to say an aspiring actor, when he and Mary were married for two short years immediately after college. Steiner felt he had defeated Philip in their unspoken battle because Steiner was married to Mary for much longer—thus proving himself more resilient, if nothing else—and because he and Mary had produced a child, which, Steiner felt vaguely, was nature's idea of a human being's primary duty upon the Earth. So he experienced not a tinge of jealousy whenever Philip's name came up. Until this precise moment.

The *Tribune* story was about Philip's current employer, the World Health Organization, and its work with AIDS patients in Africa. Philip had given up on acting when he reached the age of thirty-five, even though he'd been on Broadway in substantial but not starring roles, and had been cast in maybe a dozen Hollywood films. Philip enrolled in the School of International Affairs at Columbia, and began a new career. The *Tribune* photograph showed Philip speaking with a stricken-looking Ethiopian woman who was holding an infant. There was something staged and sentimental about the picture, but like so many correctly executed publicity shots, it sent a clear message: Philip was there to help them. The article quoted him at some length, but Steiner was mildly consoled to discover that Philip was featured not because his work was exceptional, but because it was emblematic of the work done by WHO. The PR people likely picked Philip because he was handsome and smart enough, a good spokesman who never took a bad picture and had a full head of hair. And Steiner had to admit it, Philip was cute: he looked at the African woman in the photo with a toned-down version of the subtle grin he'd used all his life to get what he wanted from pretty girls or anyone else who crossed his path.

Still, Philip had become a citizen of the world, a status available only to those whose work transcended national borders: artists, scholars, soldiers, diplomats, sophisticated criminals, big deal businessmen, drunken journalists, certain athletes, terrorists, and the like. Meanwhile, Steiner felt like a mere citizen of his own little world, a provincial of the self on the Upper East Side. Had Mary and Philip stayed together, they could have traveled throughout Africa with Philip saving lives and Mary recruiting African authors as her company bled money and won more and more grants and awards, although—who knows?—one day she probably would have stumbled on some genius whose oversexed writing would make her fortune.

Steiner gave Philip credit for this: he had changed his life, which definitely earned him points in Mary's estimation, too. Yes, this was transformation—and very impressive, Steiner had to admit. Philip likely brought to his new profession his native intelligence and his actor's ability to dominate a room. His superb posture was on display in the *Tribune* photo, too: back straight, chest out, head held properly high. All that training at Julliard had paid off. Anyone who carried himself that well couldn't be all that bad in the sack. It was one of those passing notions Steiner instantly promised to erase from his mind, though he'd fail, of course. Philip was now and forever filed away in Steiner's mind as a great lay.

"I should have gone back to school like Philip," Steiner said.

"Why are you always bringing it back to yourself?" Mary said. "The article isn't about you."

Steiner said nothing. Why fight? Fights start, and then they are forgotten or pushed away. Why bother? It was so tiresome for Steiner to have to stand up for himself. He loathed doing it as much as Mary loathed what she called the unchanging, unexamined behavior that provoked her.

Château Rouge, their stop, was three stations away.

Steiner tried and failed to read about the latest actions by the French investigative judge who'd been assigned great powers to arrest and interrogate suspected terrorists whenever he pleased. Steiner had followed the judge's story, and he rooted for him with the same ardent innocence that Michael used to root for the good guy at the movies. The French had a tradition of powerful investigative judges, larger-than-life creatures big enough for a Balzac novel. Who's the guy in Balzac, Steiner more or less asked himself—the one who finally gets Balzac's beloved villain Vautrin?

Names, it is universally acknowledged by anyone over the age of forty, disappear from memory at the first onset of middle age. Mary knew by now to introduce herself to anyone who said hello to Steiner in the street because Steiner almost surely would not remember the person's name. During Mary's rare visits to Steiner's office—had she been there more than twice?—Steiner walked the floor where all the producers sat in order to rehearse the introductions: "Christina, this is my wife Mary. ...Hey Maria, this is Mary, my wife..."

What was the name of the investigative judge who gets Vautrin at the end of *A Harlot High and Low*—as *Splendeurs et Misères des Courtisanes* is for some reason called in its Penguin English language edition? His name started with the letter "C." Steiner encountered him first in *Cousin Pons,* but the character was slightly different in that novel. It was the judge's wife who was the real mastermind of poor Pons' financial ruin. Balzac created so many characters that he sometimes got them confused or changed them as he created the *Human Comedy*. Balzac died at the age of fifty-one, just a couple of years older than Steiner. His collected letters exceeded his published works in length—which made Steiner imagine two piles of books, each taller than himself, stacked next to each other in Balzac's house on the rue Raynouard, now the lovely little Maison de Balzac which Mary referred to as Steiner's church. He and Mary absolutely had to go back there if they were going to be anywhere near Passy.

The interrogation of Vautrin took place in the jail cells beneath the Île de la Cité, cells that were still there. When Steiner visited Paris with Michael, they'd waited in line outside the *Palais de Justice*. The exhibition inside the *Conciegerie* featured a badly produced videotape about the French Revolution. Its production value brought to mind the sleep-inducing sixteen-millimeter educational films Steiner's high school teachers sometimes showed. But Michael was thrilled to visit the actual bloody scene of the very Stalinist-style French Terror.

That jail is where Steiner's imagination placed the suspected terrorists today as he happily imagined an imposing French judge, sharp and vicious, scaring the living shit out of Arab suspects. It was an ugly, racist little fantasy, Steiner realized, but he didn't think it was uncharacteristic of the imaginings of his fellow citizens.

Steiner had tried to get Michael to read Balzac, but the boy entirely ignored his father's literary advice. Which is exactly what Steiner himself did when he failed to read *Catch-22* after Murray, his own father, told him it was the most realistic account of the cynicism and absurdity of World War II. Steiner hadn't read *Catch-22* to this day, though a few years back, he did finally read Heller's *Something Happened*, which Steiner told Mary was the definitive account of the selfishness of men of his father's generation. Mary responded by never reading *Something Happened*, payback, Steiner thought, for his own failure to read the titles that his wife published. Thus the tragic cycle of literary boycotts continued within Steiner's half-literate little family.

So many gaps, so little knowledge: Steiner's ignorance weighed on him now that he realized that most of it would never be remedied. He'd never hold the basic narrative of French history in his head, and he couldn't even name all of the regimes that ruled France during Balzac's lifetime. Let's see, immediately after the French Revolution… Oh fuck it.

Camusot, that's the name of Balzac's judge. Steiner finally thought of the name. It was Camusot who won a confession from Balzac's arch criminal Vautrin. Camusot somehow got smarter and freed himself from the domination of his bitch of a wife somewhere between *Cousin Pons* and *A Harlot High and Low*. Well, good for him.

"Sit up," Mary told Steiner, as he—he guessed—slumped over his pages of the paper. Sulking at his wife's critique of his posture and what felt like her rebuke of—well, of who he was—Steiner sucked in his stomach and tried to point his chest towards the heavens, sitting like he imagined Philip was sitting somewhere in Ethiopia.

58

Though Steiner tried to avoid generalizations about the differences between the French and Americans, he couldn't help but notice that there definitely were more readers—and more readers of books rather than newspapers or magazines—in the Paris Metro than in the New York City subway where so many of Steiner's fellow New Yorkers unashamedly stared into space or, perhaps, contemplated their dreams—which is what Steiner himself was doing.

Last night, his second in Paris, after a dinner of pleasantly fatty duck *confit* and a chilled red Bourgeuil from the Loire Valley, Steiner slept as deeply as an exhausted child, and he dreamed a familiar dream. Steiner believed that dreams might be random neurological firings, what the mind did to rid itself of excess impulses as it rested, getting ready for another novel-length day of human consciousness. The notion that dreams offered a path to understanding the unconscious mind, as Mary thought in her Jungian way, felt to Steiner like a shortcut to enlightenment. Yet certain dreams presented themselves again and again. If only he could decode them, he might know something new.

As Steiner slept next to his wife on the small bed in the guest room of his friend's apartment on the Boulevard Saint Germain where the Christmas lights, Mary was happy to report, shut off at eleven to conserve energy and not disturb anyone's sleep, Steiner dreamed that he floated just above the East River, gliding happily under the 59th Street Bridge. In the dream, the great river was alive with everybody's favorites—tugboats—along with sailboats, and kayaks, what you'd see near a resort rather than a big city. Then somewhere south of the Brooklyn Bridge, Steiner saw a little village. Whitewashed shacks stood along the shore. Maybe fishermen used them as a place to clean and gut their fish, and some were used by beach-goers on vacation. Here was a small fishing town right there in New York City. The hills—so rare in Manhattan—climbed gently from the shore, leading to uncrowded bars and restaurants where people sat outside drinking their beer. Suddenly Steiner was back on land, walking the winding streets that looked more like a Greek port town than New York City, though the bars and shops that lined them were city bars, familiar-looking places. What a great little discovery, a seaside town right here on the shores of Manhattan.

Why hadn't Steiner heard about this before? He had to tell Mary. How could they go back?

The dreams always ended before Steiner wanted them to, so great was his pleasure, his feeling of having arrived in an enchanted place as vivid as the first appreciation of spring he remembered from his youth—the first time he understood why everyone made such a big deal about the smell of flowers, the sound of the birds, the first rays of warm sun across one's face.

Mary would know what the dream meant, or she at least wouldn't hesitate to offer a Jungian interpretation, but Steiner was in no mood to risk it as they rode beneath Paris in silence. Mary used to tell Steiner her dreams, sometimes at great length, and they were really something: violent and compelling and filled with witches, hit men, fires she couldn't escape from, mysterious creatures who wanted to kill her. They were the stuff of fairy tales or action-packed blockbuster movies with special effects. But Steiner usually found Mary's dreams as boring as the big, noisy, action-packed summer movies his son used to force him to endure. Tell a dream, Henry James observed somewhere, and you lose a reader.

Their stop had come: Château Rouge.

"Don't throw away that article about Philip," Mary said, taking the *Tribune* from Steiner and placing it in the large black Prada carryall he'd bought for her that summer, the one she took to her shoemaker who charged $30 to remove the metal Prada label from the side of the bag. "When they start putting my books in Prada stores, I'll start wearing their logo all over town," Mary declared.

As they climbed the endless stairs leading from the Metro to the street, Steiner told his wife, "I've never been jealous of Philip before now—because he's never really accomplished anything."

"Truly?" Mary said. "You're truly jealous?"

"A bit."

"Oh darling,' Mary said with a laugh, taking his hand for a moment.

"Well, Philip is pretty good-looking, isn't he?" Steiner asked.

"Yes he is."

"That's not what you're supposed to say."

"What am I supposed to say?"

"You know."

"But you are much better-looking," Mary said.

"No, I'm not," Steiner said dourly, though he actually believed that he might be.

Less than twelve hours earlier, they'd again made love—or had sex or whatever it was—in Tad and Judith's guestroom, after Steiner surprised himself upon emerging from the shower when he enticed Mary into briefly allowing him to approach her from behind as she bent over the sink. That lasted for a little while before, in the perfect privacy of their spacious Parisian sanctuary, they headed to the guest bedroom for a more conventional resolution of the issue. As he left the bathroom, Steiner briefly caught of a glimpse of himself in the full-length mirror inside the door, raising the question: How does a forty-nine-year-old man in pretty good shape look with an erection? Not too good to Steiner's eyes, though he was really not a connoisseur of the genre.

Given the mood between Steiner and Mary as they labored up yet another hill, climbing toward Sacré Coeur, the memory of the bathroom seemed distant indeed. Strange how long-married couples can go from intimacy to grim silence over the course of a few hours. The sun comes out, the clouds roll in—such was marriage, at least that's what it was like in Steiner's view as he faced the rue de Poulet, or Chicken Street, as Mary called it when she was in a better mood. Steiner could think of no jokes he had not made eight months earlier and twelve months before that, the last two times they'd walked across the rue de Poulet. Steiner felt like shit: upset stomach, fatigue, headache—which, come to think of it, even Steiner would admit, was how he usually felt on an average day in New York City. He could never travel to Africa to help people the way Philip did. Steiner himself needed help whenever he left the Left Bank or the island of Manhattan.

Compared with Tad and Judith's chillingly homogenous, well-groomed neighborhood, the northern part of Paris really was strikingly New York-like in its clashing styles and ethnic mix. It was also less well maintained than Saint Germain des Prés. The central arrondissements were subsidized by the taxes paid by all Frenchmen, or so Steiner had read once in the *Times*. The famously precious and aesthetically pleasing parts of the city were constantly groomed by countless street sweepers with their optimistic lime green trucks and brooms, as well as an army of gardeners who planted, pruned and replanted the thousands of flowers in the Tuilleries and Luxemboug Gardens. So the center of Paris was like a giant stage set constantly fussed over by the most diligent set dressers and stagehands in Europe. Perhaps the contrast between rich and poor seemed greater in Paris than New York because in Paris the rich had a greater gift for being rich—they did it without apology. Poorer Parisians were largely pushed to the outlying arrondissements or the crime-and-drug filled housing projects that encircled the city like a guilty conscience, just as housing projects surrounded Manhattan.

Steiner and Mary were in African Paris now, a neighborhood populated by lean but smoothly muscled types who dressed in bright blue, orange, and yellow patterned dashikis, the women with impressive head wraps that made them even taller, almost monumental. The spices coming from the restaurants and stores, the incense, and the bodies, too—none of it smelled like the seventh arrondissement. It smelled worse, to Steiner's delicate nose at least. But different noses liked different smells; even Steiner had learned that after forty-nine years of living the thin slice of life he lived on the thin slice of Manhattan and the thin slice of the Western world where he nearly felt at home.

The small markets they passed next seemed to be Moroccan. There sure were a lot of Arabs in Paris. That's one reason the French were keeping their distance from this upcoming American war, Steiner thought. If these people hate America now, imagine how they'll feel in a couple of months when the million-dollar cruise missiles start landing on Baghdad.

Steiner decided to tell Mary about his dream.

"Do you have that dream a lot?" she asked, after listening—with what to Steiner seemed like unfeigned interest—to his account of floating around Manhattan and stumbling upon an undiscovered little gem of a village on its very shores.

"Two or three times a year, I don't know," Steiner said. "Sometimes it's set in Paris or Venice, but it's basically the same dream."

"You know what I think it's about?"

"No idea."

"I think it's about hope," Mary said in her most delicate voice, the one he loved best.

"Really?" Steiner said? "It's about hope?"

It was not a word he'd associated with himself recently—or ever, come to think of it. Nor was it a word he currently associated with his country or the new century, the last one he'd see.

"It shows that you're still looking for a beautiful place—your psyche is still capable of imagining a balanced, productive life. It's very optimistic."

"No, really?"

"Really."

It was —Steiner himself could think of no other way to put it—as if the clouds had parted, though this was Paris in December, and of course a cold drizzle had just begun to fall from the dark, sullen sky.

Steiner put up his umbrella and took his wife's hand as they climbed slowly up a hill, up the stairs, and up still another hill on what was, let's face it, their very scenic walk through the Utrillo painting—to name an artist no one ever mentioned anymore—that led up to his old friends' familiar, pleasantly disheveled three-bedroom apartment.

For the past few years, when coming north to see Johnny and his family, Steiner had felt like a rich American visiting his unrich bohemian Parisian friends—certainly an accurate summary of the situation. "Look," Steiner told Johnny on the phone the last time he and Mary were in Paris, "I know you don't want to go to the Closerie des Lilas because you think it's a tourist trap because it's been famous for so long, but I happen to like the place, and so does my buddy Gilles— and he's lived in the neighborhood his whole life. And dinner is on me, so let's just go there. If we sit on the glassed-in terrace on Sunday night, I guarantee you'll see mostly French families with little kids and old couples from the neighborhood."

Though Steiner's bossy tone was a recent acquisition, a carryover from corporate life, the standard he'd used with Johnny hearkened back to the way the friends had always judged Parisian restaurants, cafés, even doctors' offices: if too many Americans were there, you were in the wrong place. The two were only twenty when they devised that litmus test, yet Steiner adhered to it still. It was foolishness, he knew, but even now if Americans were seated next to him in a restaurant in Paris or he heard English from across the room, he felt defeated, as if he'd come all this way to find something different, but had ended up in a coffee shop on the corner of 93rd and Broadway, a block away from where he'd grown up. Yet what was wrong with being an American in Paris? What was wrong with being who he was or being among people just like him doing exactly what he was doing?

Steiner and Johnny met when they were students together. Johnny, the only American in their junior year abroad program who didn't favor dungarees in 1975, was standing by the board that listed rooms for rent. With his dirty blond cropped hair, khaki pants, work boots, and aging T-shirt, Johnny looked more 1950s than 1970s. He smoked an unfiltered cigarette and stared at the smoke he exhaled with the sort of serious interest most men reserve for a woman they're trying to seduce. Johnny's T-shirt was a dull red like the brick of an old New York building. Steiner always missed that distinct New York color when he spent too much time in Paris where buildings made entirely of brick were rare. The worn pinkish orange brick of the ancient Places des Vosges was more delicate and beautifully frail: compared with American brick, it was feminine in some mysterious way.

That name—Johnny—to Steiner it had always been suspect. John C. Ward, Jr., to use Johnny's full name, had by 1975 made the self-conscious decision to hold onto the nickname his family started using when he was in grade school. It had helped to distinguish him from his father, and he continued to use it as an adult living in France. Had Johnny Ward spelled his first name with a final "ie" rather than a "y" back in Illinois? Steiner suspected it, but so what? Johnny was nearly famous within the world of European avant-garde theater. He was the father of five. He'd earned the right to be called whatever he pleased.

Johnny was handsome with sharp features—a sculpted nose, fair skin, straight teeth by virtue of either good luck or a good orthodontist. And Johnny was fit. He'd been a champion swimmer at college before quitting the team to hang out in the theater department because he preferred to think of himself as a creative type, an artist, as he boasted without embarrassment. Besides, the theater department was where all the pretty girls were.

The son of a father who ran the insurance company his own father had founded, Johnny possessed the self-assurance and social poise of a young man who'd soaked up all the benefits of being raised as an elite member of a manageably small society where everyone knew, liked, and feared his father. So Johnny quite naturally behaved as if Paris was a small town where everyone knew and liked him, and of course, this became a self-fulfilling prophesy: most people, French and American, liked Johnny, and everyone used the nickname that instantly made them feel they knew him better than they really did.

In 1975, of course, Steiner knew none of this about Johnny's background. When they met that day in Paris—it must have been in early September—Johnny told Steiner about a *chambre de bonne* that was too expensive for Johnny's budget. Johnny had seen the place, but he couldn't afford it. Poor kid, Steiner thought, his parents don't have any dough. To Steiner the room sounded great, and it's where he wound up staying. Johnny, living according to a self-imposed pledge to support himself to some extent, moved to the obscure, charmless tenth arrondissement, north of Gare de l'Est. But Steiner stayed in the sixth, happily whittling away at the money from the check he'd taken from his father's hand in New York before getting into a cab and heading for the JFK airport, humming the Marseillaise to keep up his courage.

After Steiner read Balzac's *Colonel Chabert* years later, he associated Johnny's apartment near the Canal Saint Martin with the impoverished rural quarters where Chabert, Balzac's Napoleonic hero manqué, lived after returning to Paris and discovering that his wife had remarried and refused to acknowledge Chabert as the husband whose heroic death on the battlefield had been reported years before. For Steiner, *Colonel Chabert* was the tale of a worldly man undone by a worldlier woman because the old soldier possessed the more innocent heart. The man of action is ultimately naïve compared to the selfish wife whose character he misjudged. Steiner found the story consoling. He cherished the thought that he might be wiser about women than more aggressive types like Chabert: he hoped that he would turn out to be stronger than at present he seemed to be.

Johnny did keep one foot in the sixth by taking a job as a dishwasher, a *plongeur*. It delighted Johnny, the child of so much privilege and good luck, to be paid forty francs a day by Didier, the owner of the storefront restaurant where Steiner ate his solitary dinner six nights a week. That Didier paid his dishwasher by banging four ten-franc pieces on the counter after each night's work delighted Johnny, who told Steiner, "I think Didier gets a kick out of paying an America with coins." Eventually, Didier invited Johnny to join him and the Basque waiter for their weekly Saturday night drink at the tiny working man's bar across from the Marché Saint Germain. Johnny was thrilled to be initiated into this all-male proletariat institution. When Steiner passed the crowded bar at around eleven one night and saw Johnny inside drinking with Didier, Steiner was jealous as he rarely had been in his life.

Each time that he visited Paris in the years to come, Steiner walked past the bar just to make sure it was still there. This was typical of his behavior: he always returned to the same places, noting how they'd changed, and telling himself the old stories—though they were not even stories, really, more like mere incidents or tableaus. It was if Steiner might somehow change their outcome—move backwards in time and maybe introduce some action, some plot.

Johnny had done better. Seeking a more authentic life, Johnny succeeding in having a more authentically Parisian existence than Steiner. But Johnny's room in the tenth had no bath, and he had to share a toilet with his fellow lodgers. The not unclean toilet was located down the hall from Johnny's small, sunless room on the rue du Faubourg Saint Martin. Once a week Johnny journeyed to the public baths, and the rest of the time, he stank.

"I smell like a Frenchman on the Metro," Johnny would say with a smile. But Johnny's odor was worse than the much-commented-upon normal Frenchman's body odor: it was the sort of human stench that can only be accumulated over time. In those days, Johnny was likely the smelliest upper-middle-class American kid in Paris. Well, that was something accomplished.

Johnny often invited himself over to Steiner's place, so that when Steiner's aging landlady wasn't looking, Johnny could sneak in for a quick bath. Steiner adored the old woman who, after he'd known her for a few months, showed him the fake identity cards she still kept from the days when she was a young Jewish woman hiding from the Nazis. There must have been ten cards stored away in the table beside her bed, each with a different name and the same unsmiling black-and-white photo of her thirty-year-old self. The landlady's name was Madame Vatel, like the chef to Louis XIV, she always said. Vatel was her husband's name, and it was only because of his help that she was able to evade the Gestapo. Each day at 11:30 in the morning, Monsieur Vatel, a retired lawyer, dressed in a suit and tie, walked their dog—a Daschund named Marsha, which Madame always described as "*un nom Américain.*" At the café on the corner, the Pré Saint Germain, Monsieur Vatel would stand at the bar with Marsha on her leash at his side, and with great dignity drink "*un demi,*" a small glass of blond beer.

Steiner loved the old couple, and they'd been very generous with him, inviting him for oysters and champagne, so that he did not have to spend Christmas Eve alone. But mostly he loved Madame Vatel for the way she spoke to him slowly in French, gossiping and informing him about the neighborhood while correcting his pronunciation in ways that never made him feel like shit.

So Steiner felt particularly bad whenever he helped Johnny sneak in to use the bath, especially because warm water was the one thing Madame was cheap about, though she was otherwise free of the petty penny-pinching that so often afflicts the elderly no matter how much money they have. But in Madame's mind, hot water was more expensive than the liters of Evian or the bottles of good Bordeaux Steiner could not help but notice she and her husband drank with dinner each night.

One day after his bath, Johnny, still stinking slightly in his khakis and sleeveless white undershirt, reached into his pocket, pulled out a joint, and said to Steiner, "You don't mind if I light up, do you?" But Steiner did mind, he minded because—imagine how quaint this was in 1975—it was *illegal* and Steiner then, as now, did not believe in breaking the law.

"You can't do that here," he told Johnny.

Murray Steiner had been an assistant district attorney before going into private practice, and while Murray's political opinions were standard

67

issue Upper West Side liberal, he believed in obeying the law, not fucking with the police. Besides, Murray had a friend in the Police Benevolent Association, so he'd made a bit of money defending cops over the years. In 1968 or '69, Steiner wasn't sure which, Murray was in the front seat of a cab taking a group of Steiner's friends to an anti-war rally, when a cop directing traffic held up his hand to stop the cabby from making a turn. The cabby, a pony-tailed hippie, probably a pot smoker now that Steiner thought about it, muttered, "God damned pig," to which Murray responded, "New York City cops are not pigs. They're the best cops in America." Steiner's friends laughed to themselves in the back seat, and Steiner felt embarrassed, but in the years to come the comment became a source of pride for the way Steiner's old man had had the presence of mind to precisely correct the unexamined rhetoric of the moment, stand apart from the spirit of the times.

Johnny, however, all but laughed in Steiner's face when Steiner refused to let him light up the joint in his room in Paris in 1975, and while the friends had stayed close, Steiner always sensed that somehow the smirk never fully left Johnny's face. Steiner was definitely more of an establishmentarian than his friend who'd benefited so much from being born into what used to be called the Establishment, back when the phrase was used as a term of derision by young people who didn't quite understand the benefits of artfully kissing ass.

Johnny stayed on in Paris after his junior year. He took a year off and worked as a clown, a performer in a touring theater troupe that traveled around France and North Africa. Johnny went back to the States to finish college, and then returned to Paris where he married the actress girlfriend he'd met on the road.

Claire was a smart and tough girl from Marseille. Beautiful, too, of course. They both smoked cigarettes—American, not French, for some reason—before the five kids came, then they stopped, though Claire smoked sometimes in the morning, just one cigarette. Claire looked as Italian as she did French with her dark curly hair cut short now and her olive skin. To be pretty and genuinely feminine with such short hair was to be a pretty woman indeed. Claire's English was grammatically perfect, and she actually read many of the books Mary published, particularly the ones about Jungian psychology. Claire even read the natural healing stuff—which had such surprisingly large and enduring sales—and she seemed to believe what she read.

The lives Johnny and Claire lived in Paris would be unimaginable in America, and Johnny knew it. He even celebrated it. Johnny's theatrical productions were financed by the State. Claire worked as a stage manager in Johnny's shows and commercial productions all over Paris. "She's one of the best stage managers in town," Johnny reported. But when either of them were out of work, the unemployment compensation was generous. And now Johnny's plays were appearing at least once a year in Paris, in bigger theaters each time, and Johnny had twice been invited to direct his work in Tokyo and had a growing following in Germany and Spain.

Johnny had likely heard the talk about France being finished as a creative and intellectual center, but he'd ignored it and done just as he pleased. He learned the language, toured the country, and learned a trade—the theater—from the ground up. He'd gotten the girl, had his kids, and raised them as Frenchmen, Frenchmen who spoke English like little stage Frenchmen, with the corniest and most endearing accents. True, Johnny had family money, help from home to fall back on, but as far as Steiner knew, Johnny hadn't taken a dime from Dad since graduating from college.

Johnny was even prescient enough to understand that up there—just a five-minute walk from the honky tonk awfulness around Sacré Coeur that Steiner and Mary were now passing through—was the thriving little village of Montmartre with an indigenous population who climbed up and down the hills and lived on beautiful blocks where the air actually felt a whiff cleaner and rents were more affordable than in central Paris. Catching his breath, Steiner guessed that the citizens of Montmartre were surely the most aerobically fit in all of Paris.

To Mary, the abandon of Johnny and Claire's approach to life was the opposite of worried. To be more specific, it was the opposite of Steiner's worrying, just as the cheerful disarray of Johnny and Claire's Montmartre apartment was the opposite of the dust-free order Steiner strived for on the Upper East Side, especially after Michael had gone off to school.

Johnny and Claire were two of Mary's favorites, and though Steiner, of course, had known them both longer, Mary took over the upkeep of the couples' friendship. While Steiner sometimes didn't open his friends' e-mails or letters for a week after they arrived, Mary always kept in touch promptly. Mary particularly admired the optimism with which they were raising five children on their very bohemian income. While Mary and Steiner were fretting about whether to have a second child, Johnny and Claire were as fecund as—well—as New York City public school students, to make the sort of joke that Steiner would never make in his wife's presence, or Johnny and Claire's, either.

Johnny, whose circumstances growing up were even more cushioned than Steiner's own admittedly cushy circumstances, had lived a more fearless life than his friend Steiner, and Steiner knew it. But Mary, she shoved it in Steiner's face, he felt, and this was pissing him off quite a bit as Johnny, smiling that handsome American grin, opened the door to his messy apartment and announced, "Guess what? Dinner's on me. I've been waiting to tell you this in person, but I won one of those genius awards. I won a MacArthur."

⁘ FIVE ⁘

L ike the good director—no the *genius*—the world now agreed he was, Johnny had chosen the restaurant well. It was a location, to use the show biz term, that embodied the character of the star of the evening—Johnny himself—while also dramatizing the differences between the star and the second male lead, our friend Steiner, who very quickly downed his second glass of Loire valley red—which was becoming the official wine of this visit to Paris.

Johnny must have done a location survey, Steiner thought, because, as Johnny knew, this dark mirrored joint on the rue Lepic was just the sort of place Steiner liked. The red of the exterior made Steiner instantly feel at home in a way he couldn't begin to explain, as did the sight of the long zinc bar crowded with older French men. What were the storefronts of Parisian restaurants made from anyway? Cast iron, was Steiner's best guess. Or maybe it was wood covered with thick layers of high gloss paint. Steiner didn't know. And why did the sight of bars with aging, reddish exteriors make him feel welcome whether he saw them in New York, Dublin, London, Amsterdam, or Paris, though never in LA where the bars or restaurants never seemed like anything other than theatrical stage sets, which, come to think of it, was what bars and restaurants were, anyway?

As they pressed their way through the masculine milieu at the restaurant's entrance, Steiner remembered the question Mary had posed that morning when she and Steiner left the Musée d'Orsay, a building that had been an abandoned train station when Steiner was a student. In those days, most of the Renoirs, Monets, Manets, Pissaros, and Cézannes in Paris—paintings that somehow seemed less exhausted by their fame back then—were housed in the Jeu de Paume where you didn't have to wait in line for over an hour to walk in the front door. When Mary asked Steiner to name his favorite painting at the museum, admittedly not the most discerning question Mary had ever posed, he heard himself say, "Cézanne's 'The Card Players'" without really thinking it through.

"Why do you suppose that is?" Mary asked, seeking psychological insight.

"It's a very specific place, a very serious, very specifically masculine scene," Steiner said, trying to please his wife, of course, but also curious to understand the painting's allure.

"So you respond to the content of a painting," Mary said, "subject matter rather than form."

This was true, Steiner readily admitted. His experience of paintings, especially in recent years, had become detached from the small amount of training in art history he'd had as an undergraduate. He saw content, not form. This made him, he knew, as philistine as those who read a novel for story rather than language, but he was not a specialist in the visual arts, and it's just the way he had come to absorb paintings. Mary, who had learned from her father, saw form first. Well, she was philistine elsewhere, Steiner assured himself, though he couldn't really name those places.

But now, as he took in the scene at the bar on the rue Lepic and felt the entirely agreeable effect of two glasses of Saumur on his very empty stomach, Steiner thought he knew why he was drawn, albeit in an uncultivated way, to the men in the Cézanne: they reminded him of the men in the bar where Didier took Johnny. After three decades, Steiner was still intrigued by this glimpse of the initiation scene: Johnny at the bar with Didier. Back in college when Steiner was studying Henry James, a professor told the assembled nineteen-year-olds, "The unlived life is a peculiarly American phenomenon." Ain't it the truth?

"The whole time I've lived in France I've never had pig's feet," Johnny reported after turning over the reassuringly uninventive, very traditional menu—exactly the sort of *carte* Steiner liked best.

"Neither have I," said Steiner, who prided himself on eating almost anything French that sounded disgusting, from the green salad tossed with fried pig's ears he'd found rather tasty a few years back, to the blood sausage, *andouilette*, and *rillettes de porc* he ate routinely without suffering serious intestinal symptoms.

"Don't eat pig's feet to celebrate your MacArthur," Mary said, sounding just like she did when she told Michael years ago not to use his finger to push his food onto his fork. And it worked on Johnny, too: he picked up the menu, looking for a new choice.

"Maybe I'll order the pig's feet," Steiner said to Johnny. "I'm so amazingly jealous that you've won this thing that I'll get sick tonight anyway, so I might as well eat something grotesque."

"That's why I love you," Johnny told Steiner somewhat theatrically—a professional hazard for directors, of course. "Because you're so fucking honest. A French person would never say that—even as a joke."

"Because it's true," Steiner said.

"Yup, yup, that's why they'd never say it."

Johnny was being gracious to the unemployed American who was only now discovering that a ballsier, riskier route to fame and fortune— for that is exactly what Steiner understood Johnny's goals for himself to be—was, in fact, a superior strategy.

There was no doubt about it, for the first time in years, Johnny's stock was higher than Steiner's, as was Mary's first husband's, come to think of it. When human beings reach middle age, Mary's doctor had told her, their parts shrink: woman's breasts get smaller and men's penises, too. This was the worst news from the medical world that Steiner had heard in years. His own sexual organ felt numb now, as it often did, but to the extent that it had any sensation at all, it felt small. Johnny Ward was buying dinner for Steiner for the first time in over ten years, probably twenty. This, as much as anything else in the recent history of the world, made Steiner feel as though he was wrong about everything: the way he spent each moment of his waking life fretting about all the wrong things. He felt like he had absolutely nothing to say. Was this overwhelming humility Steiner was experiencing? Or was it humiliation? He didn't really know the difference right now, but he thought he might never speak again.

"What's this wine?" Johnny asked. "It's great."

Johnny had never cultivated a taste for good food, good wine, nice clothes, creature comforts of any kind. Now that he'd been given all that money by the MacArthur people—more than the value of the stock options Steiner had worked so hard for and so stupidly failed to cash in—perhaps Johnny would buy himself a nice suit. For years Johnny used to dress in Steiner's hand-me-downs, and Steiner's annual Parisian dinners with Johnny took on an uncanny air, with Johnny showing up in, say, the brown Brooks Brothers tweed jacket Mary had finally made Steiner give away, while Johnny's feet would be in the hand-made brown wingtips Steiner had paid a fortune for in London. He and Johnny were the same age, but when he saw Johnny in his old clothes Steiner sometimes felt like he was hanging out with a younger version of himself. But if Johnny suddenly began wearing new and expensive suits, studying the wine list and selecting the perfect under-rated Bordeaux—that really would be too much.

"It's a Saumur," Steiner heard himself say.

Another sentence formed in his head and Steiner found that he could speak it out loud.

"Do you know which Balzac novel takes places in Saumur?" he asked.

"I do," Mary said.

"Eugénie Grandet," Johnny said with very impressive intonation, though Claire quickly repeated the title in a far more melodious fashion which just made Steiner think, Oh shit, I'll never really learn this fucking language.

"That's correct," Steiner said. "So you've been reading Balzac?"

"Thanks to you," Johnny said. "In fact, my next production is a stage adaptation of *Colonel Chabert.*"

"I gave you that book in English."

"That's right," Johnny said.

"I told you to turn it into a play."

"You did?"

"Yes. It was my idea. I should be the executive producer. That's what I do for a living: I have ideas like that. I want my ten percent."

"You got it," Johnny said, laughing. "We're mixing up the text, a wonderful French composer is doing the incidental music, and I think I'll use video and television monitors again. Maybe I'll do it in modern dress. The new designer for Balenciaga is actually from Saumur. I met him at a party, and he offered to do the costumes. He's a wonderful designer. He invited us to one of his fashion shows under the tents at the Tuilleries. But I'm not sure about the costumes yet. I want the production to be like a nightmare—like Chabert's nightmare life. That's my idea for now. It's still at the workshop stage. But I have a contract to do it here in Paris and then bring it to Japan next fall, so I better get cracking."

"And there's a chance of a small European tour as well," Claire said. "But they really love Johnny's work in Tokyo. His production there last year was a big success."

"Let me know when you're going there," Mary said. "I have to schedule a trip to Tokyo next fall, so maybe we can hook up."

"That would be great," Johnny said.

"What's Balenciaga?" Steiner asked, feeling like a depressed housewife who never gets to go anywhere while her executive husband travels the world, doing deals and discreetly procuring the services of high-priced hookers known only to concierges at the best hotels.

"Balenciaga is a great fashion house that's having a huge resurgence," Mary said.

"You know, I was thinking that you're really like Chabert," Johnny said, after everyone had ordered their dinner, and Johnny had asked for another bottle of Saumur and then engaged in what to Steiner, in his current mood, seemed like an exaggeratedly prolonged chat with the waiter about pig's feet which Johnny finally ordered in unspoken defiance of Mary. Such was the power of a MacArthur to make a man trust his instincts.

"Oh for Christ's sake," Steiner said. "I really don't see myself as being like Chabert."

"No, I'm serious," Johnny said, and Steiner saw that Johnny had become a man who conceived that his whims were always worth exploring. Like Steiner, Johnny had grown used to being the boss, used to the respectful silence that came when he indulged himself by thinking out loud.

"In what way," Steiner asked, "am I like a dignified and heroic Napoleonic soldier who digs himself out from beneath a pile of dead bodies on a battlefield, wanders in exile, and returns to Paris to reclaim his wealth and his woman—only to be outmaneuvered by his worldly wife?"

Mary and Claire exchanged glances that indicated that they'd both like to leave the table where their egocentric husbands were engaging in cryptic masculine communications. Left on their own, the women could speak directly about important feminine matters without silly games.

"Well, think about your position," Johnny said. "You commanded a group of people, you won awards—just like Chabert won his medals. And now your company has tossed you out, just like Chabert was ostracized by a society that no longer needed soldiers. You're a commander without troops..."

"But my wife hasn't left me and taken my money," Steiner said.

"Give me time, darling," Mary said.

"Oh my," Claire said with a nervous giggle that made Steiner guess that perhaps wives in Paris don't break their husbands balls quite like this.

"My life might be a farce," Steiner said, "but it's not a tragedy, and I'm not a hero, am I darling?"

"You're my hero," Mary said in a mocking but not unwarm tone.

"My life is comic, not tragic," Steiner said, "because it's going to have a happy ending, though I have absolutely no idea what it's going to be."

"That's your problem," Johnny said, actually pointing his finger at Steiner. "You never took yourself seriously enough."

"That is not his problem," Mary said.

Was she defending her husband? Steiner couldn't tell.

"Okay," Johnny said, trying again, "your problem is that you're such an optimist. You're such an American."

"Those," said Steiner, "are two things I don't think I've ever been accused of, but I have to tell you there are worse things in the world to be."

This got a laugh, though Steiner guessed that perhaps he was the only person present who understood the degree to which he really wasn't kidding at all.

"Well, I wanted this to be a surprise," Johnny told Steiner with a puckishly pleased expression. "But I'm going to dedicate the Chabert production to you. I think it'll say something like, 'To my American friend who introduced me to Balzac.' I hope you'll come to the opening. It's in May here in Paris. What do you think?"

What did Steiner think? He didn't know. He didn't know if he'd want to spend the money in April—after all, he might still not have a job. The world might be in the middle of a very ugly war. Steiner was touched, of course, that Johnny intended to dedicate the production to him, but Steiner sensed that his friend was magnanimously presenting the runner-up trophy in the race they'd been silently running against each other for all these years. Their competition was a bit like the *Tour de France*: it took place in a foreign country, Steiner didn't really follow it very carefully, and he'd never fully understood the rules. But now it was clear that he'd lost.

"That's wonderful, Johnny," Mary said. "We'll definitely try to come. That would be lovely."

"I'm touched, really, Johnny," Steiner said. "I love *Colonel Chabert*, though I don't think of it as a commentary on my own life. Some of it took place near this neighborhood, didn't it? That farm Chabert lived in was up near the Canal St. Martin where you used to live in that stinky little apartment, remember?"

"I've heard about that little apartment," Claire said fondly. "It's become a legend."

"Hearing it is one thing," Steiner said. "But I smelled it."

"No, you're wrong," Johnny said with assurance and that touch of a lingering smile that offended Steiner so much.

"What am I wrong about?"

"About Chabert. I've read it a hundred times now in French and in English. Colonel Chabert's wife lived in her second husband's mansion on the rue de Varennes where the Musée Rodin is today. She had a monkey for a pet. The dairy farm where the lawyer visits Chabert later in the novel was in the Faubourg Saint Marceau, which is the same neighborhood as Ma Vanquer's boarding house is in *Le Père Goriot*. Believe me, I'm right about this. I've been living and breathing Balzac for the past few months, looking for the right piece to adapt."

"Are you sure?" Steiner said. "The boarding house in *Goriot* is down by Val de Grâce."

"Yup, yup, yup, I'm absolutely sure," Johnny said.

77

"Well, what do I know?" Steiner said. "I don't even remember the monkey."

"Yup, yup, yup, there is a monkey," Johnny said again merrily, as Steiner observed that his friend's English had become a bit eccentric from all the time abroad. "When the lawyer goes to see Chabert's wife, there's a pet monkey hopping around in the background. It was very prestigious to keep an exotic animal like that in the Faubourg Saint Germain in those days. I don't know how to handle that, but I was thinking it might be fun to either have a video loop of a monkey on stage—or maybe a live monkey. There's a bear in the book, too. Do you remember it?"

"I don't remember anything," Steiner said. "I'm a TV producer. I don't know anything; just ask my wife."

"No, no, no, it's not true," Mary said, as if she'd never made her husband feel illiterate compared to her.

"The soldier who takes Chabert in runs a dairy farm," Johnny continued, "but Balzac says the old sergeant also makes money from the trained bears that he owns. I think trained bears were a phenomenon in Paris in Balzac's time, but I have to do more research. There was a theater in the sixth where you always stay—the *Théâtre des Deux Pigeons* on the rue Clement near where you used to live. It was close to where the soup kitchen is now. Someone told me there used to be a famous dancing bear at the theater. I'm not sure I believe it."

"Bears in Paris in the sixth arrondissement, no, I don't think so," Claire said. "We have the honey bees in the Luxembourg Gardens maybe..."

"It's starting to sound like a Disney production," Steiner said.

"Oh no," Claire said, mortified. "Don't say that."

How tiresome it must be for Claire to be married to man who'd long hoped he was a genius only to be officially declared one at the midpoint of his life. Johnny might never shut up again, and Claire might be forced to spend the rest of her life in beautiful, unspeaking admiration. Well, Steiner knew what a huge boost to the ego it was to be in charge of large productions: everyone asks you a million questions, from what color the scenery should be painted to what a performer should do with her hands. And few men endure a steady diet of that kind of power without coming to think that their instincts are correct about absolutely everything.

Though Claire had been married to Steiner's friend for close to twenty years, Steiner didn't know her all that well. She was not an American, of course, which created more of a barrier than Steiner had imagined when she married Johnny. And she wasn't entirely French, either: with her dark features and Italian father, she was more the effortlessly sexy Italian type. Claire and Steiner had never spent more than three minutes alone together, he guessed, and only during moments when Johnny had yet to arrive at a café or Johnny and Mary had walked ahead on the street, say, and Steiner found himself filling the silence by posing questions to her. Claire looked great tonight in her thick gray turtleneck, cotton rather than wool because of the mild winter, and Steiner noticed that her cheeks and pretty hands held onto a summer tan. Steiner felt a kinship with Claire. Their jobs were provincial compared to their spouses' work: Claire came into contact with Parisian theater people, and Steiner always worked with the same group of New York television professionals he'd known for years. Meanwhile, Mary and Johnny's careers put them on a sort of slow-motion perpetual world tour.

"Is Balzac prized today in France?" Steiner asked Claire. "Do kids study him? Did you when you were young?"

"Oh no," she said, like a chic Parisian schoolgirl dismissing an unappealing pullover while shopping with a friend. "I think we read maybe *Le Père Goriot*, I don't remember. Johnny is the one who is the Balzac man now. There is the statue by Rodin. But to us now in France Balzac is not someone we think too often about."

How had Claire managed to have five kids, work exhausting hours, and keep her figure?

"You look great, Claire," Steiner said.

"Oh you know," she said, dismissing the flattery.

"It's that book," Johnny said with a laugh. "That diet book—*The Best Diet*, by that designer—what's his name?"

"Lagerfeld," Claire said. "Karl Lagerfeld."

"We saw it in the stores," Mary said.

"Oh it's everywhere," Claire added with a smile. "And it works. Lagerfeld, he was so fat, grotesque with that fan he used to carry all the time. He was killing himself. Now he looks better, but still too skinny—like an American girl. But I am glad for him. It is better for his health. He will live longer and create more beauty. A friend took me to a show he did for Chanel. So beautiful. Truly an art. He has a store near you in Saint Germain, for another of his lines. It is Gallery Lagerfeld on the rue Jacob. You should go there, Mary. Very sophisticated clothes. Very expensive, but I think they would be your style."

This was the most Claire had said at dinner thus far, and Steiner was glad to see her flush subtly with enthusiasm. Did Steiner believe that fashion was art? Oh, what did it matter?

The second bottle of Saumur arrived, already opened and slightly chilled. Steiner looked away and took in the French couple at the next table who ate their dinner while engaging in what seemed like an intimate conversation interrupted by very skilled kisses.

"To all of our children," Mary said as they all clinked glasses. Steiner held his glass by the stem so that the sound of glass against glass would be more melodic. Who taught him to do that? It was actually Claire one night years ago.

"And how are the kids?" Mary asked, which made Steiner feel rude for not inquiring earlier.

"Great, just great," Johnny said. "And my old man will be glad he doesn't have to pay for their schools for a while—thanks to the MacArthur."

"What?" Steiner asked in an outraged voice that surprised all present. "What?"

"Who do you think was paying all those private school bills?" Claire asked with a laugh. "Not us. Not on our salaries. Half of the time we are on *chomage*—unemployment."

"No? Really? I had no idea," Steiner said. "Well, we have that in common: I'm collecting unemployment now, too."

"Not me," Johnny said with a laugh. "I don't think I qualify anymore because of this goddamned grant."

"And what are the children up to?" Mary asked.

"Oh they are good," Claire said, before rattling off the list of where each of the five were going to school. Their eldest was headed for the

École Normale Superior. "He will go into business, I think," Claire said. "Or government."

"He'll probably end up running an American corporation," Johnny said.

"There are worse things in life," Steiner said distantly.

"Oh no," Claire said. "We really can't think there are many. After 9/11, we all—most people here in France—felt very bad for the Americans. And you in New York, your courage was very beautiful right after it happened, but now, with this war in Iraq…"

"For the record, I didn't display an ounce of courage on 9/11," Steiner said. "I just watched television and worried."

"Michael is going to an anti-war rally with his friends from school," Mary reported.

"Good, good, good," Johnny said.

"Yes, we all will march," Claire said with a weariness that to Steiner felt very French. "And that book that you published, Mary, it was very brilliant. We all liked it very much. But what will come of any of it? In a few days, everyone will get their Christmas presents like always, and then in February or March will come the war. And the American soldiers will be killed, and the Iraqi children will die from the American bombs that your taxes pay for—and Johnny's, too. We can do nothing."

Steiner did not wish to have a conversation in which all assembled agreed on the folly of American foreign policy, nor did he wish to expose the fact that he had not read the tiny book Mary published to such acclaim and financial reward even though reading the damn thing would take him less than three hours.

"And since 9/11," Johnny asked, "how much has New York changed? We haven't been there in two years. Where were you guys when it happened again?"

Steiner definitely did not want to tell those stories again. They'd gone through it with Johnny and Claire in Paris last spring. Had Johnny forgotten? In New York, 9/11 had become a sort of overused conversation starter. The subject made those New Yorkers who'd survived feel fully alive: it was serious; involved history; and carried a consoling message for Steiner and his wealthy friends who were reassured to know that cops and firefighters—astonishingly courageous strangers—

81

would risk their lives to save them. The whole tragic narrative became for many a cloistered version of a war story.

"Oh I don't want to talk about 9/11," Steiner said with the sort of annoyance he usually only displayed in front of his own family. "We went over all that when we were here in April."

"Yes, you are right," Claire said.

Steiner instantly regretted his sullen tone. He really was becoming a grumpy son of a bitch. The couple that had been making out next to them had vanished—off to get laid, no doubt, but the waiters' faces showed nothing beyond professional detachment as they cleared the lovers' dishes from the table. Steiner hoped for a trace of a smile from the men, unspoken admiration for all that impressive kissing. But the waiters just went about their business, and Steiner thought of indifferent cemetery workers covering a casket with earth once the weeping family leaves a graveside. But then again, he was in a very bad mood.

Just after Thanksgiving, Steiner saw Ground Zero for the first time. He'd just had lunch with a friend who worked on Wall Street, a banker whose long-time pot dealer worked in a mailroom in Tower Two where he died. Steiner hadn't wanted to see the blocks of death which were quickly transforming from a disaster area to a shrine, a tourist attraction. But it seemed cowardly in the end to avoid the site of the profound wound to the bottom of the island where Steiner had lived almost all of his life. Besides, without a job, Steiner no longer had an excuse to spare himself: he had nothing else to do after lunch.

A few workers lingered at the bottom of the astonishingly large crater. You really can't tell how big something is when you see it only on TV, Steiner reminded himself: it's a horribly inadequate medium for conveying what anything is really like—a ball field, a beautiful woman, or a scene of devastation. He doubted that anyone clearing the vast, now officially sacred sight that day was indifferent. Or so Steiner imagined on the rue Lepic in his half-drunken reverie as he watched the waiters quickly reset the neighboring table with a dispassionate air.

Claire was correct: the attack had inspired something very beautiful, true, and courageous. But what did Steiner know about truth or beauty or courage? The events of 9/11 had brought out the best in many New Yorkers, many Americans. Yet what awaited his fellow countrymen now, Steiner feared, was more death, more graves. And Claire was correct also, Steiner thought, when she said that nothing that Mary could do with her books or Michael could do with his protests—or anyone could do with their dinner table conversation—would change all the violence that was coming the world's way very soon.

~ SIX ~

They walked in darkness down the Boulevard Saint Germain before seven on Christmas morning. The slight drizzle was not serious by the standards of Parisian winters, which Steiner remembered as nothing but cold and dank. It was warm, too. The temperature would again be in the low fifties. The great deserted Boulevard was slick and black. They had been extraordinarily lucky with the weather, and Steiner realized how much it helped his mood.

He had worried that he and Mary wouldn't be able to get a cab on Christmas morning, but a half dozen taxis waited at the stand near the Lipp, their diesel engines purring like patient, happy cats. It was a reassuring noise, as was the stealthy crunch of the heavy door closing inside the cab and the moneyed, oily scent of its tan leather seats. If Steiner had ever been in a cleaner taxi, he couldn't remember it. How did Parisian cabbies afford such fancy cars? In New York, the cabs were shit, but you could put out your hand at most corners and find one.

Steiner and his wife absorbed the steely silence of their chauffeured Mercedes as they headed west, past the Musée de Cluny where Steiner had never ventured in all these years; past what used to be the Café Cluny but was now a fast-food joint; and past the fifth arrondissement stores with the well-made, distinctly French pens and notebooks Steiner used to be able to get only in Paris, though he could now buy them in half the stationery stores on Madison Avenue.

And there finally was Chez René, the restaurant where, almost three decades ago, Steiner had used the credit card his father gave him for "emergencies only" to take his German girlfriend out to a farewell dinner. That was in the late spring. The portly French businessman dining alone across from the young couple drank an entire bottle of Bordeaux while eating his springtime feast of *asperges vinaigrette* followed by lamb with *flageolets*. After a suitable pause, the fellow ordered the cheese plate, and then a *tarte tartin* followed by an after-dinner Cognac. The man swayed slightly in his 1970s-style three-piece suit when he left the restaurant, but managed to keep his dignity as the waiters sent him away with the usual elaborate salutation given to regular customers.

At dinner that night, Gitta was still trying to convince Steiner to come with her to Berlin where she planned to work as a waitress for the summer before returning to her studies. Having spent a year at the École des Beaux Arts, she decided that she really wanted to be a doctor. Smart girl, better a doctor than the failed artist she was, statistically speaking, very likely to become.

"I do not want to end up teaching art to brats in Munich," Gitta said, because she was afraid she'd end up doing exactly what her mother had done for a living. She and Steiner could have stayed in Gitta's sister's apartment in Berlin. "It has air conditioning," she told Steiner, trying to appeal to his American sensibility. Steiner and Gitta had spent more than two months together, holding hands, seeing movies, drinking coffee, and having sex. Why on earth didn't Steiner accept her offer to go to Berlin? Which of those activities did he not enjoy? What stopped him? Well, Germany wasn't terribly appealing to a young Jew in those days. Just over thirty years earlier, Germans of Gitta's parents' generation had shot at Steiner's father. Gitta's own father, she told Steiner early on, was drafted into the German army and quickly captured by the British. He spent most of World War II in a British prison camp, she said. But Steiner always wondered if the story was true: it seemed almost tailor-made to appeal to his Jewish-American prejudices. Now Gitta wanted Steiner to come to Berlin, the city where in 1945 Murray Steiner, then a German-speaking GI, had stood guard over the former Fuhrer Bunker.

In the quiet cab Steiner, seated with his wife a few inches away, could remember only one thing he didn't like about Gitta: she had terrible taste in literature and was always trying to get him to read contemporary American writers he couldn't stand. One more thing: Gitta really wanted Steiner to fuck her up the ass, but he couldn't make himself do it. He was a good boy from the Upper West Side, and it just seemed so unsanitary—and besides, he didn't feel the impulse. Up there? No way, thought Steiner who, as instructed by his mother, washed his hands after every one of the thousands and thousands of subway rides he'd ever taken in his life. "You can wear a condom," Gitta said, discussing the matter with an unembarrassed practicality that awed Steiner. But Steiner never sodomized the intelligent, lovely, obliging, good-natured, long-legged, and flat-assed Gitta. As he reconsidered the issue decades later while he crossed the Seine in a cab with his wife at his side, he accused himself of having been an idiot back then. And an idiot right now, come to think of it.

"It's Christmas Day," Mary reminded Steiner with the air of a patient but stern instructor. "Does this day mean anything to you?"

There was something pissy in Mary's tone, even though they'd made love the evening before. It was as if she'd only just figured out that her husband was not a Christian. Usually, when they had the sort of sexual rally they'd been staging here in Paris, Mary's considerable edges were a bit smoothed out, but not on this particular Christmas morning.

"Christmas means something to me," Steiner protested, though he was still engaged in a vague erotic daydream set in Gitta's small, crumbling studio on the rue Notre Dame des Champs and involving, of course, anal intercourse. How bad could it have been? Updike seemed to write about it with enthusiasm, and Mailer, too. Those old guys must know something. What a coward he was. Given the chance now...

"No, I'm curious," Mary continued. "Does today feel at all special to you, or is it just like every other day?"

Well, clearly Christmas meant more to Mary, having been raised Catholic, just as it surely did to Gitta who, now that Steiner thought of it, definitely would have made a good deal of very exciting noise if Steiner had buggered her, as he absolutely should have done. Perhaps if she hadn't been German, it would have been easier. But the cultural taboo of a Jewish boy having an affair with a German girl combined with the sexual taboo in question was too much even for Steiner, a third generation atheist. Who knows, though, maybe Murray got up to a bit of buggery with those *frauleins* back in Berlin. But there were some things that even Steiner didn't wish to contemplate on the holiest day of the Christian calendar. Or was that Easter? Probably Easter, at least in Mary's view, though what did she know? She hadn't attended mass once in all the time Steiner knew her.

Steiner's own family exchanged Christmas presents, as did a few of the other deracinated Jews in his almost entirely Jewish West End Avenue building. Years later, though, Steiner noted—and not entirely without pleasure—the unexpressed shock on his parents' faces the first time they saw the Christmas tree that Mary continued to insist upon putting in the living room each December. Neither of Steiner's parents said a word, but they seemed especially displeased to learn that Michael genuinely enjoyed decorating the tree with the ornaments mother and son made together each Christmas. The green totem made Mary happy in the way that kippered salmon on a bagel pleased Murray Steiner, to mix the sacred and the profane in a way that Mary would find unamusing if not offensive because kippered salmon held no spiritual meaning. Steiner himself tolerated the tree and took pleasure in the pleasure it gave to Mary, but he worried about the green needles that dropped all over the living room, hiding in the corners and under the sofa until April or May. To Mary, this was merely a metaphor for her husband's deeper anxieties about the non-practicing Christian half of his household.

Steiner hoped that Michael would remember to water Mary's tree back in New York. Otherwise, the floor would be covered with those goddamned needles. Well, at least his son would be with friends on Christmas, well brought-up kids who'd try not to destroy Steiner's apartment during the free-floating, politically correct orgy that surely would accompany their righteous protest against American foreign policy. Would Michael take any pleasure at the sight of the Christmas tree? Would he point out that he and his mother had made the ornament near the top—the one with the photo of his late, lamented mutt Sinbad, the pet Michael loved so much, and a very great dog indeed? Mary would try to get him on the phone later.

Fashions in Jewishness had changed since Steiner was a kid, and now many of Steiner's friends, who—like Steiner—had never been *bar mitzvahed*, sent their kids to Hebrew school and even showed up at synagogue on the High Holy Days. To be a proud atheist like Steiner was suddenly to be "ashamed of being Jewish," though Steiner dismissed the whole topic as if it were the sad remnant of another century, outdated superstition, as Murray would put it. It bothered Steiner that American Jews were becoming more Jewish, Israeli fanatics were becoming more fanatical, American Christians were becoming more Christian, Muslims were becoming more Muslim, and the whole world seemed to be regressing into religious mania, when Steiner would have guessed it would evolve in the opposite direction as a new century began. If everyone would just behave exactly and precisely like him, all of these stupid problems would go away.

Steiner's own memories of Christmas were utterly unambiguous: he liked everything about the way his family celebrated the religion-free holiday as a sort of annual winter retail festival.

On Christmas mornings, when Steiner was a boy, he was always selfishly delighted to find that a fresh supply of what he would now consider to be junk had been stuffed into his father's black knee-high dress sock that Steiner had hung the night before. Chocolate Santas, candy canes, tiny model cars, and once a toy electric razor—Steiner loved it all, especially the razor with the fake electric buzz that he used to pretend he was shaving just like his father. Steiner remembered the feel of Murray's beard when he gave his father a kiss. How long had it been since Steiner last felt it? Many men Steiner's age made a show of kissing their old man, and saying "Dad, I love you." Not Steiner. Murray had resumed his paternal kisses in recent years, but Steiner didn't kiss back. It seemed like such a sentimental cliché. He knew Murray longed for it in his unspoken, severe way, but Steiner just couldn't oblige him. And he hadn't called his father "Dad" or even "Father" in years. What did Steiner call him? Murray never seemed quite right, though it was how Steiner referred to his father when he wrote in his date book. It was easy to call Lola "Mother" still, but Murray just didn't seem like "Dad." In person, Steiner actually avoided calling Murray anything at all, evading the need to name his old man the same way stutterers learn to circumnavigate words they find particularly difficult to pronounce. Steiner was no longer much interested in being a son. Murray, as far as he was concerned, had blown his many chances to be much of a father. When Murray got the bill for Steiner's farewell dinner with Gitta, Murray complained that the credit card he'd given his son was to be used exclusively for emergencies. "I only used it once all year," Steiner said, though Murray responded with a lawyerly, "We had an agreement, and you violated it." Steiner hated his father's cheapness. Steiner bought Michael anything the boy wanted, and as a result Michael wanted very little: he was the opposite of spoiled.

Just as Steiner accused Mary of compensating for her self-indulgent father by being such a hard ass, Mary suggested that he'd become a TV executive to correct the injustice that had been done to his mother when Lola was fired from her job doing commentary on a local New York TV station when Steiner was at the impressionable age of thirteen. It really was the worst thing that happened to his mother in Steiner's lifetime— and she never entirely recovered. Lola was never as well-known or happy again, and she spent the rest of her life shopping, reading the *Times*, writing a column for a West Side newspaper that was given away for free, and formulating opinions that she insisted were more interesting than anything on local TV—which really didn't take much. After Lola had been off the air for a year or so, people stopped recognizing her in the famous food markets on Broadway that Steiner hadn't patronized for years because he found them so nervous-making, so filled with the unsettling and hysterical quest for the perfect piece of cheese. "You want to undo the wrong that was done to your mother," Mary told her husband. "That's why you went into TV—and that's why you ended up in management. You want to prove that you would have been a better protector than your father."

Maybe Mary was correct. But Steiner believed that dwelling on his own childhood was regressive, even morbid. For Steiner, childhood was like a TV show that had been wrapped. He liked to think he was working on new projects, even though at present, he couldn't help but remember, he was unemployed.

Because it was Christmas and Steiner did not wish to be seen as a parsimonious non-Christian—and did not wish to feel like the cheap son of a cheap father—he tipped the taxi driver an extra ten percent, wished him a Merry Christmas, and received an outsized *"merci monsieur"* in return.

Steiner's relationships with the strangers he over-tipped were, he sometimes thought, the most honest relationships in his life: they were openly and entirely about money. But why did he care what cabbies, waiters, bellhops, barbers, and other strangers thought of him? Not only here in France, but in America, too. Well, perhaps everyone cares. Or perhaps he cared too much. Steiner didn't know which was closer to the truth, though he felt proud to follow in the tradition of great over-tippers like Sartre, Joyce, and the countless mobsters he read about and saw in movies and on TV.

The Gare de Lyon, still majestic with the nineteenth-century notion that travel was a significant undertaking, was close to deserted when they arrived. The Train Bleu, that great museum of a restaurant, was closed. A handful of travelers, many by themselves, headed for dutiful half-day visits to their provincial families, or so Steiner surmised. The day-trippers looked at their tickets and then looked up at the departure board, checking and rechecking their track location. Strange how travel can turn adults into insecure children, worried that they'll miss the train they see waiting only ten feet away. Steiner thought of all the Balzac provincials who came to Paris from the country to make their fortune and test their talents: there was Rastignac, of course, Lucien de Rubempré. Who else? Steiner couldn't think of one name. All those hours with Penguin Classics in hand and his forty-nine-year-old mind came up blank. This was more bad news that he would not report to his wife.

The newspaper stand at the train station was already open, and Mary bought *Le Monde,* which had replaced *Libération* as her official Parisian paper now that *Le Monde* had given her book ink on the front page. Well, there were worse traits in a woman than gratitude.

It was still dark when their less-than-half-full train started its journey south towards Burgundy beneath a cloudy sky, but soon the gray gloom lifted and a dull pink winter sun rose over what to Steiner seemed like the self-consciously scenic hills between the lovely little towns. Actually, they *were* self-consciously scenic, come to think of it: the French government subsidized farmers, partly to make sure that there'd always be a great view when you crossed France by train. Or so Steiner thought he remembered reading a long time ago. The train itself was sort of a broken-down mess that smelled of stale urine. So much for the idea that all European trains were brand new, though this one was still nicer than the clanking, often-tardy relic Steiner sometimes took to Connecticut late on a Friday night.

"Beautiful" was all Steiner could think to say whenever Mary nudged him to look up from the previous day's *Herald Tribune* to take in the rolling hills and small towns, though Mary's expression seemed to challenge him to do better.

The newspaper reported that a French cameraman had been killed in an accident while riding alongside an American tank training in the Kuwaiti dessert. The guy was hanging out of a jeep, trying to get a great shot. From the brief description, Steiner, who revered good cameramen, guessed the poor fellow might have been too ambitious for his own good. Imagine dying because you had a creative idea, tried to execute it, and then—catastrophe. That's not the last time something like that's going to happen in the Middle East in the coming months, Steiner guessed, and he wondered if Tad and Judith were being sufficiently careful. Well, it was hard to be careful when people were shooting at you, though Murray told Steiner that the first thing infantrymen did during World War II was figure out how not to get killed—while also not looking like a coward in front of their fellow soldiers. "No one wanted to embarrass themselves," Murray said. Fear of embarrassment was certainly an underrated force in human history. Did Steiner even begin to understand the feeling of embarrassment that overwhelmed him so often? No. Absolutely not. Even Steiner would admit that to himself, though not to Mary. Some things were just too embarrassing to talk about, even with your beloved, difficult wife.

Steiner wondered how much it affected his view of himself that his father had behaved with dignity in combat, while he had not had the chance to see how he'd do. Balzac, who—fortunately—missed the opportunity to get killed for his hero Napoleon, fawned over soldiers in his novels, but never got past writing the first few pages of his own attempt at a war novel. It was one of Balzac's few false starts.

"My secret was that I was young and stupid," Murray told Steiner. "I didn't think I could die. The old guys, the married guys—forget about it. They thought about things too much. We didn't even make friends with them when they came up to the front because we knew they'd get killed."

That Murray—then a skinny, nineteen-year-old provincial from Brooklyn who'd never knowingly met a non-Jew before going into the army—performed bravely, was a continuing source of pride to Steiner. It also pleased him to recall that Murray reported it was usually the tough guys—"the hillbillies and football players," as Murray derisively put it—who broke down. "World War II was the best thing that ever happened to me," Murray said. "Combat is great, as long as you don't get shot."

Well, if World War II was pretty great for Murray, it was pretty great for his son, too. If Murray hadn't been a soldier, the GI Bill would not have paid for his law school and he would not have earned enough money to send his bookish son to the private grammar school that helped Steiner pass the test to get into the elite public high school that led to that impressive college in New England where Steiner always suspected he might not have been admitted if his father hadn't been able to pay the full tuition. World War II allowed Steiner to have a childhood which he estimated was more privileged than ninety-five percent of his fellow countrymen. The war also allowed Steiner to go to Paris where he met the friend whose country house he'd soon visit if this clanking relic of a train ever got to where it was going.

And soon enough a brand new, very real war would be unfolding in front of America's eyes—unfolding on TV. And part of Steiner looked forward to watching it in the same way that he looked forward to watching the baseball playoffs each fall when the Yankees contended for the championship: it was a bit of excitement, something to do at night. It would be good TV. No, great TV.

Steiner, of course, was ashamed to covet the cozy pleasure of sitting inviolably on the sofa, remote control in hand, somehow exhilarated by live images of people halfway around the world killing and being killed. Yes, it would be a lot like watching sports. Why had the idea of being a devout sports fan achieved universal approbation in America? Why was it good to be a die-hard fan? Well, sports were a harmless distraction whereas the coming war, that was very real. And if you saw something on TV, Steiner knew, you felt like you were seeing it, but you really couldn't see—or understand it—correctly. TV viewers could not comprehend the violence they witnessed because it would all be packaged so extremely well.

"Make sure the packaging is good," Bill Fuller always told Steiner when Steiner was developing a new show. So Steiner learned to spend much of his budget on graphics—show openings, animated effects, the teases that ran just before the commercial breaks. Steiner knew that these highly produced moments at the beginning and end of each segment—the "edges" of a show—were what interested Bill Fuller the most. With Bill as his boss, Steiner learned the importance of packaging over content; he discovered how most people watch TV. Which was also how he guessed most people would watch the war.

Watch the war. At news stations around the world, promos were already being prepared: "Catch all the action live, as it happens, right here on…"

Gilles, as promised, was waiting for Steiner and Mary at the tiny sand-colored stone train station. Was that ivy growing up the side of the building? Was ivy still green in winter? Steiner wasn't sure.

Gracious was not a word that came easily to Steiner, but he felt Gilles was genuinely that. Gilles had the good fortune to have been born in one of the best neighborhoods in the world, the southern end of the fifth arrondissement of Paris, and he then had the good sense to stay there for the rest of his life. Gilles grew up near Val de Grâce. It was a neighborhood Steiner now more than ever associated with Balzac, given the news that Johnny reported about where, in fact, Colonel Chabert's friend's farm actually was. Gilles was raised with his brother in a huge apartment on the rue Claude Bernard, equidistant between the Luxembourg Gardens and the Mouffetard Market. His parents were both attorneys. The family was Jewish, and had lost dozens of relatives in the Holocaust. Gilles' grandmother, a concentration camp survivor, was turned in to the Gestapo by her concierge, teaching her family an abiding lesson, of course, about what it means to be a Jew in French society, or, more broadly, what it means to be a human being on the planet Earth. The old lady survived the camps and was still living, and Gilles was devoted to her, yet still funny on the subject of her eccentricities. Steiner spoke with her at Gilles' wedding, and she was impressively patient, inquiring about life in New York in slow-paced, Russian-accented French that Steiner could easily follow. Hard to imagine that the blue eyes that had seen two concentration camps were now seeing her grandson marry an Irish woman.

Gilles' surviving family thrived after the war. Early on, he and his brother were identified as brilliant by the French educational establishment, and the paths were cleared for them to succeed. But they really did more than that; they excelled. Gilles' younger brother, a graduate of the École Normale Supérieur, a few blocks from his childhood home, was close to being famous as a business executive. During his annual visits, Steiner would hear from Gilles: Olivier is now the number three economist at the World Bank, or number two at the Bourse. "He has a car and driver standing by at all times waiting for him," Gilles reported. In the spring, Gilles' wife told Mary, "Olivier has become the most desirable dinner guest in Paris." What exactly had Olivier done to achieve this status? Steiner hadn't seen Olivier since Gilles' wedding when Olivier managed to look elegant and unselfconscious in a bright green cotton suit from Yves Saint Laurent. "I should get a green suit," Steiner told Mary, who replied, "You should, but you never will." But a month before they were married, Mary presented Steiner with a similar Saint Laurent suit in a luminous bright blue, rather than green, because as Mary observed, "I don't want to look at photos of you in a green suit for the rest of my life." The gift still hung in his closet wrapped in dry cleaner's plastic, a cherished memory into which he could not quite squeeze his slowly broadening middle-aged self.

As for Gilles, he moved easily from the Sorbonne to medical school. He was among the elite of the internationally known experts on obesity and diabetes, definitely a burgeoning field in the very fat Western World. Gilles' achievements did not bring him the gaudy income they would in the United States, but fortunately for Gilles, his Dublin-born wife Jean had recently become rich by writing mysteries. Very literate mysteries that got good reviews in the *Times*, and were sometimes made into films or movies for cable television channels with artistic aspirations. Mary had read two, and reported that they were excellent. Steiner never read mysteries. He had actually never read one page of any of Jean's work, and he sometimes cringed at the thought that Jean might one day discover this. When Mary asked why Steiner didn't just read one of the short, breezy books, Steiner replied that mysteries were a waste of time. "And you don't waste time?" Mary asked.

Conversation with Gilles was about his profession, his family, food, international relations, or practical matters like the cost of apartments in Paris as opposed to New York, the remodeling of his country house, and the like. He was also immensely fond of jokes; especially jokes about Jews, which he told with great success in his accented English. Asked to compare the practice of medicine in France and America, where Gilles had interned for a year, Gilles said, "In America, if the surgeon leaves the sponge in the patient, the patient sues for a million dollars. In France, the doctor tells the patient, 'You are so stupid that you must have done something to make me leave the sponge inside of you.' And the patient must apologize to the doctor."

After Gilles married Jean, they took an apartment two blocks from his family's place. If Gilles found the proximity to his parents oppressive, he didn't report it. After Jean's career took off, they bought a larger apartment around the corner from the old place. When Gilles walked to work at the hospital in the mornings, he passed his childhood home, his college, and his medical school. So through the luck of being born in the right place and being blessed with an excellent intellect and disposition, Gilles had the confidence of the small-town boy who excels together with the cosmopolitan polish of a sophisticated Parisian. He had a thriving career as the head of a lab five minutes from his apartment; a beautiful and successful wife; two daughters and a young son, all of whom could only be described as beautiful; and, of course, wealth. Was he happy? Absolutely and without guilt or self-consciousness. Gilles was glad to be who he was. He literally held his head up high.

The warm grin on Gilles' face as he caught sight of Steiner and Mary at the tiny train station suggested that Gilles was a man who had everything, whereas Steiner was a man who had just lost his job and was worried if he'd worn the right shoes.

What does one wear when invited to the French countryside for Christmas day *en famille*? This was an issue for Mary, though Steiner offered one thought: waterproof shoes. He was right about that, he saw,

95

as he walked along the muddy path that ran parallel to the railroad tracks. The somewhat practical, black, rubber-souled Prada boots Mary had been so pleased with when she purchased them in New York a month ago were covered with wet mud, as were Steiner's black waterproof Timberlands.

"Don't look down," Mary said when she caught Steiner gazing at his own feet. "You're in a beautiful place. Look up. Watch Gilles: do what he does."

Looking up is precisely what Gilles was doing right now, as he stood smiling like a proud mayor of a small town greeting his constituents at an annual festival. Without derision, Mary often said that Gilles' bulbous, Gallic nose was phallic, and pronounced it quite sexy. Which Gilles certainly was, as far as Steiner could tell: curly blonde hair, now slightly gray and cut short; pale blue eyes; muscular arms, and a broad back and chest, though these days Gilles exercised hardly at all. In recent years, Gilles had gained a bit of weight, and Steiner liked to tease him about it.

"It's okay," Gilles said easily, "I am an ectomorph. I have good genes. I can lose it easily after the holidays."

Such was the collected wisdom about obesity that Gilles had gathered during medical school, years of research, and a lifetime of attending conferences on the subject all over the globe. Besides, the small belly was sort of becoming on Gilles: it reinforced the image of a proud French papa, which Gilles certainly was.

Early on in his first stay in Paris, Steiner met Gilles on the tennis courts at the Luxembourg Gardens. Gilles had watched Steiner easily defeating a fellow American student, and Gilles more or less challenged Steiner to a match. Steiner had noticed how oddly passive Frenchmen were when they played tennis: most of them didn't even keep score, they just rallied back and forth and enjoyed being outdoors in the park. So he looked at Gilles and instantly thought: I can beat this guy.

Steiner and Gilles were soon playing tennis twice a week in almost complete silence and with utter seriousness. They played in the park until the end of November, Thanksgiving Day in the States, when they were the only ones on the courts. The hard part was holding onto the racquet in the cold. The only words they exchanged during the matches were the score and information about whether the shots were in or out. Steiner quickly learned the handful of words he needed for his French tennis vocabulary, shouting "*égalité*," "*avantage*," "*jeu*," "*set*," and "*match*" across the net. The sets were always extremely close, though Gilles won five sets for every one that Steiner did. Still, Steiner didn't remember ever being routed. Steiner's big American serve and forehand usually fell to Gilles' deliberate, correct ground strokes. Gilles won because he was a more well-rounded player with no serious flaws in his game, except perhaps for a weak second serve, while Steiner's game had one obvious weakness which Gilles exploited mercilessly: Steiner never developed a solid backhand. These days, Steiner could hit a top-spin backhand down the line, but back then he couldn't; and it never occurred to him to try to learn a new stroke to replace the lame slice he'd learned when he was twelve.

Though players were only supposed to play on the courts for an hour at a time, Gilles told Steiner not to worry when their matches went on for up to two hours. "We are the best players here," Gilles said. "No one will say anything." Well, this was France, and they *were* the aristocrats of the courts—which carried certain privileges. It was a small demonstration of the power of insouciance, and over the years Steiner watched with admiration as the same approach worked for Gilles in restaurants, clothing stores, and with women on both sides of the Atlantic.

Gilles could no longer play tennis because of a bad back, but when he visited Steiner's summer house a couple of years earlier, the two played hours of grueling Ping-Pong matches, with Gilles again winning more often than not. But once again the matches were so competitive that Steiner didn't mind losing. The pure stupid sweaty fun of playing a game with a friend in the basement in the July heat reminded Steiner of his youth, and he'd never felt closer to Gilles.

Steiner and Gilles literally came from the same place: their grandparents were Russian Jews. Yet their expressions differed, not only because of their differing natures, but also because of the language they spoke and where they lived. Gilles exhibited the full range of predictable Gallic shrugs and the habit of dismissively puckering his lips and exhaling when he disapproved of something. But Mary also singled out Gilles' way of tilting his head up with a refined air, silently dismissing anything that displeased him. Years ago, Steiner and Mary were having dinner in a restaurant in Paris with Gilles and Jean when they ran into one of Jean's British literary agents and his girlfriend who joined the table for coffee and dessert. While consuming their after-dinner Cognacs, the British couple began to tease each other loudly and drunkenly in a series of jokes that were amusing only to them. Then the girlfriend placed her teaspoon into the communal bowl of chocolate mousse at the center of the table, ignoring the large serving spoon everyone else had used. She took a mouthful of mousse and placed her spoon back into the bowl—which was too much for Gilles. "I am sorry but you can not eat with your spoon from the bowl that serves everyone," Gilles said decisively. When the boyfriend started to argue, Gilles stood, went to the bar, settled the check, and then invited Mary and Steiner to leave with him. Gilles' lofty expression didn't seem so much to look down upon the rude couple as look above them. Gilles expected the world to be on its best behavior in his presence. And something within him often seemed to inspire the world to live up to his expectations.

The knee-high rubber boots Gilles wore at the train station were called Wellies, Steiner thought, English boots no doubt recommended by Jean. Gilles also wore what the L.L. Bean Catalogue called a barn coat. Gilles' version was dark brown and quite sturdy looking, and Steiner was genuinely curious to know where he'd gotten it. Was it French? Its rustic air fit in perfectly with the surroundings, more so than Steiner's own New Yorker-in-Paris uniform of black jeans, black cashmere turtleneck, and black leather jacket—all of which suddenly felt hopelessly urban. Mary, though, wearing her hair wound into a French twist, was more appropriate in her long black wool skirt—practical because it was very warm, and formal because it was a skirt, but not too formal because it was a thick wool with black tights underneath it. And her jacket, a recent acquisition, was something of a small triumph.

They'd purchased the jacket the day before, on Christmas Eve, at the Gallery Lagerfeld on the rue Jacob. True to Claire's word, it was just the sort of store Mary liked with its mixture of high style and street style, though the street in question was in Paris' high rent district, which is to say among the highest rent districts in the world. Steiner and Mary were the only customers in the place at four in the afternoon, and the predictably beautiful young saleswomen—aggressive and serious in the French way—spoke to Mary and Steiner in English, though Steiner for once didn't feel insulted. You have to give credit to the Parisians, Steiner thought as soon as he found a seat: this place really has an air of chic that New York would be hard-pressed to match. That the Lagerfeld Gallery's clothes were not available in America, as the sales woman—displaying excellent strategy—had volunteered as soon as she heard Mary's American accent, only added to their appeal. Here finally was stuff you couldn't buy in Manhattan. These hangers, Steiner guessed, might contain the only clothing in Paris not also available in New York, Tokyo, Los Angeles, Bal Harbor, Manhasset, and all those places one saw listed at the bottom of clothing ads in the *Times*.

Mary tried on a pair of Lagerfeld's astronomically priced, ultra-tight blue jeans, and asked her husband, "Why do you think?"

The jeans were certainly sexy, and they made Mary's ass look great, but Steiner shook his head in discreet spousal disapproval when he looked up from the copy of *Interview* magazine he'd pulled from the rack. Steiner was somehow worn out from looking at the pictures of models and celebrities he barely recognized and skimming the articles, most of which seemed to be transcripts of interviews. That's why they call it *Interview*, of course, but the ten minutes he'd spent with the publication reminded him unpleasantly of watching TV. On page five he saw a picture of Karl Lagerfeld himself, backstage at a Chanel show, looking as tanned and thin as he did on the cover of the diet book displayed in windows throughout Saint Germain.

"Try that on," Steiner told his wife, pointing to a cropped black tweed winter jacket worn by a long-legged headless black mannequin inside the store. Mary went over and inspected the price, as Steiner eyed the shape of the mannequin's legs and firm, glossy bosom. When he was an adolescent forced to wait while his mother shopped, he'd found the mannequins at Bergdorf's quite sexy, and he was glad to discover that he hadn't changed much: he sort of had the hots for the dummy whose jacket his wife was now checking out. From Mary's expression, Steiner guessed the price of the jacket was high, but not outside her usual range.

99

The salesgirl really did speak English well, and she knew how to sell expensive clothes to Americans. Was she twenty-one years old? Steiner thought perhaps younger, but very worldly and cynical about sales. Young Parisian women didn't seem to have the noticeably large-sized American breasts sported by the young women who used to work for Steiner in New York. Perhaps it was a question of nutrition or cosmetic surgery or maybe underwear. Was the salesgirl wearing any? Steiner couldn't be sure. How pleasant it was, all in all, to be sitting there vaguely aroused by so much female energy, some of it belonging to his very own wife.

Steiner put down his credit card, telling his wife to savor the experience because she was unlikely to have it again soon. Mary grabbed the receipt. When he asked her how much it cost, she said, "Didn't you look at what you signed?" But he hadn't. The jacket made them both happy, and he didn't care about the price.

Seeing Mary in her Lagerfeld here on the outskirts of Burgundy as she stood on tiptoes to kiss Gilles on both cheeks, Steiner felt conventionally proud to be married to such a beautiful woman. This must be how Gilles feels all the time, Steiner thought, except that Gilles is never troubled by the fact that he doesn't have a job.

"So here you have the medieval gates of the town," Gilles explained as they drove over the stone bridge that led from the train station to the town. "They are very famous."

Steiner stared blankly at the gates. Did he even know what medieval meant? Before the Renaissance was the best answer Steiner could come up with. Did it mean the eleventh century? Before then maybe. Somewhere in there. Steiner assumed that Gilles had had basic historical information drilled into him by the famously strict French educational system, though he could not be sure.

The main street of the town was not entirely empty on this Christmas morning, though only a few stores were open, and the good mood of the few people who bustled along the street was infectious. Like most of his fellow Americans, Steiner unthinkingly associated Christmas with England more than France. The holiday was certainly more Dickensian than Balzacian. The shop windows were decorated with gold or silver ribbons, nothing more. He didn't see a single flashing light, and the few wreathes he noticed looked homemade.

Gilles headed into the local bakery.

"Don't buy a *bûche de Noël*," Mary said. "We brought one from Paris."

"The amount of food in that house is incredible," Gilles said, and then he instructed Mary and Steiner to walk down to the river for the view of the stone bridge while he waited in line to buy bread. Did the bridge date back to the Romans? Steiner wasn't sure. And when were the Romans here anyway? Was it before Christ or after Christ? Steiner felt as if he didn't know anything anymore. Without even trying, France was reminding him that he was half-educated at best. It was good to be told the truth, Steiner knew, but he really didn't need any more bad news on this particular Christmas Day.

The pale mud color of the small river that ran through the town almost exactly matched the sand color of the bridge they'd just crossed and the façade of most of the buildings they'd passed. A dozen or so ducks floated by in the brown water, along with a family of swans. Mary picked up a discarded piece of bread and tossed it into the river. The largest swan, the father, Steiner guessed, swam over and seemed to sniff at the bread, but then swam away. Steiner took the creature's actions personally: he felt snubbed.

"It's nice, no?" Gilles asked without false modesty as he drove Mary and Steiner up the dirt road and through the doors of the pleasantly crumbling, low stone fence that surrounded his country home. The house was the same sand color as the buildings in town, but to call it a house really was misleading: it was a château, a small early nineteenth-century mansion, maybe fifty years older than what suddenly seemed like the modest Victorian shack Steiner and Mary took such pride in back home. It was amazing how many middle-class Parisians were hooked up with really impressive country homes. What looked like a barn that had been converted into a sort of guesthouse stood next to the main structure. Across the road was an apple orchard. Horses grazed in a meadow in the distance.

"The orchard is beautiful in the spring with the flowers," Gilles told them. "And the girls pick the apples and make a tart."

"Do you ride, Gilles?" Mary asked.

"No, I am not a cowboy. And I am Jewish. But the girls, they ride, yes. English style—like Jean."

Steiner was reminded that Mary never seemed more charming than when in Gilles' presence, unless of course she was kissing some writer's ass. Yet Steiner could not help but note a double standard in his wife's attitudes. That Steiner couldn't ride a horse was evidence of her husband's morbid and neurotic urban fears and lack of physical adventurousness. But when Gilles made a not terribly inventive joke about not riding, Mary laughed happily. Well, women don't really beat the crap out of a man until they've married him, Steiner thought. Besides, women always liked Gilles, and Mary was no different. After Steiner and Gilles became friends on the tennis court, Gilles ended up sleeping with the two prettiest girls in Steiner's academic program. When asked his secret for getting girls, Gilles said simply, "I am French."

There was no need to take off their muddy boots because the stone floors in Gilles' house were used to punishment. Gilles quickly slid into a pair of clogs as he called for his wife and children with a confidence that made Steiner think of the proprietor of a business summoning his staff. He called again, but no family arrived.

"You see that they obey my command," Gilles told Mary with a smile.

In Mary's bag was the formidable bottle of Bordeaux that Steiner had purchased after a fairly lengthy consultation with the two men who ran the *cave* at the Marché Saint Germain. Gilles had learned a lot about Burgundies in recent years, so Steiner chose a Bordeaux, thinking he had more room for error the further he got from Gilles' area of expertise. Gilles' seemed sufficiently impressed, and he showed the bottle to Jean as soon as the group found her in the kitchen where Jean was cooking with Catherine, her eldest daughter. Pretty, pretty, pretty. Beautiful, beautiful, beautiful. Mother and daughter were certainly those things. Here in this house on Christmas Day the abundance of good looks and good genes felt like some sort of blessing, Steiner might have said if he permitted himself such a Christian word, though if pressed he'd say it was merely good luck.

The meal, they learned, would be served at around five: wild turkey from the farmer next door with pudding, plus, to start, oysters and foie gras, provided by Gilles' best friend, an economist named Pierre who Steiner had heard about, though never met.

"You won't eat again for a week," Gilles assured them.

"I hope we're equal to the challenge," Steiner said, patting his stomach.

"You are not obese, and you have no heart disease," Gilles said. "In fact, you are too skinny, and you exercise like a maniac. So you have nothing to worry about. Why do you worry?"

Gilles called to the two youngest children from the vast living room with its high, beamed ceiling and stone walls. When no one emerged from the adjacent room where the kids were watching an American film on TV, Gilles summoned them again in a sterner tone. The twelve-year-old daughter Matilde looked directly at Gilles when she apologized for the delayed arrival. Gilles' little boy Michel just looked down shyly and grabbed his father's leg.

"We were watching a movie, Papa," Matilde said in Irish-accented English that sounded, of course, just like her mother's speech.

It was consoling to see that children somewhere could still register the same sort of slight fear at the sound of their father that Steiner himself remembered feeling whenever Murray raised his voice. Michael had been briefly afraid of Steiner until school wised him up.

Gilles lifted his little boy into the air.

"My friends have a boy named Michael just like you at home in New York," Gilles told his son.

As Gilles gave Steiner and Mary a full house tour, "beautiful, beautiful, beautiful," was all that Steiner could think to say, whereas Mary asked precise, informed questions as if she were going to have to take a test on what materials were used in the renovation of the house.

Once Mary had been assigned a task in the kitchen and had noted how impressed she was that Jean and her daughter could cook together without bickering, Gilles took a deep breath and announced, "Now we have the time to play Ping-Pong."

Which was exactly what Steiner hoped Gilles would say. For one thing, it solved the question in the back of Steiner's mind: what exactly does one do all day in the winter at friends' country home until it's time to eat? Later, on the way back to Paris, Mary would fill Steiner in on the family news that she'd get from Jean in the kitchen. Steiner preferred to hear about personal matters second hand. It was pleasantly like reading the *Times* where he learned about all the dangerous places in the world that he would never visit himself.

Almost two hours later, after what Steiner thought must have been the most engaging physical competition he'd enjoyed in months, Steiner and Gilles, carrying five bottles of precious wine, emerged from the cellar of Gilles' guesthouse, which could not have looked more perfect if the most gifted scenic designer Steiner knew spent a week working on it. The basement was constructed with stacked rocks, like a New England stone fence. This, Steiner learned, was how basements were created back in 1830, when Balzac was coming into his prime and Gilles' place was built. The dust-covered bottles of wine lay on wooden shelves lining all sides of the cellar. The Ping-Pong table was at the center, and when Steiner chased after one of Gilles' winners, Gilles warned him, "Be careful you do not break the beautiful Montrachet."

Gilles, who'd clearly been playing a lot of Ping-Pong lately, won all but the last game they played, though the score got closer as Steiner found his timing. Steiner half-suspected that Gilles had let him win one game.

Gilles trusted Steiner to carry two dusty bottles of Beaune up the stairs, while Gilles held two bottles of champagne, the label of which Steiner did not recognize, as well as a rare Alsatian white "for the foie gras."

"That was fun," Steiner said.

"Yes," Gilles said simply.

"You are very good at Ping-Pong."

"Yes," Gilles said again.

"So how are you?" Steiner asked.

"The question is how are you?" Gilles said. "Mary told me to make sure I asked."

"Don't you hate women sometimes?" Steiner said, but Gilles, his gaze fixed on the side door of his house, seemed to miss Steiner's irony, if that's what it was.

It was hard to remember that when they met, Steiner and Gilles conversed in French. But marriage to an Irish woman and daily life with perfectly bilingual children had improved Gilles English. Lately, though, Gilles' daughters seemed to relish correcting Gilles' English, pleased to find one area in which they were clearly superior to their dauntingly intelligent father.

Steiner was slightly sweaty beneath his cashmere sweater, and he worried briefly—like an old Jew in Miami Beach in winter, he told himself—about catching a chill. But he really wasn't all that uncomfortable outside without a jacket. The temperature must have been over fifty degrees. It felt more like the fall than Christmas, and with a turkey feast on the schedule, Steiner thought of Thanksgiving.

"How do you say turkey in French?" he asked.

"*Dindon*," came the answer. "It is literally 'from the West Indies.'"

As they walked along the stone path to the kitchen entrance of the house, Gilles seemed to understand that Steiner did not want to obey his wife's instructions and talk about how he was. Well, Gilles had tried to stick to the syllabus, and Steiner was touched by the effort. But who really wants to tell an old friend that things are going badly?

"So how are you finding Paris at Christmas?" Gilles asked.

"I think I've never noticed before how many white people there are in Paris," Steiner said.

"That is strange because everyone says the opposite: they notice how many Arabs there are now."

"I mean at the very center of Paris, the sixth arrondisement, the first arrondissement, the eighth."

"Well, there are the rich people and the tourists, but in the rest of the city, there are more Arabs and Africans."

"Yes, but I think the reason Americans like Paris so much—and most people would not admit it and I would not say it to Mary—is that it's filled with white people who are very good at all the silly things white people enjoy most. You know, food, fashion, architecture, adultery…"

"It's true, we are very good at those things," Gilles said. "But it is not only white people who like these things. Most people like them, too."

Gilles was correct. Sometimes Steiner's passing thoughts felt racist, and he knew that this was probably because they *were* racist. He wondered if he'd offended Gilles.

"Well, you know, France is a racist country, just like every other country," Gilles said. "In France, everyone hates the Arabs, except for the Jews, who double-hate them."

105

Both friends laughed guiltily, knowing they were getting away with talk that would piss off their wives who were innocently preparing their feast less than fifteen yards away.

"And, of course," Gilles continued, "now the French double-hate the Jews because Israel makes the Arabs so angry—which is a problem for the French because we have so many Arabs here. But you have to be careful what you say when you say bad things about the Arabs. Remember what people said about my own grandparents right here in France: kill the Jew. That is not so far from the things I hear normal people say easily about Arabs at the hospital every day. I prefer to speak about individuals—not groups."

Gilles was correct, Steiner knew. Raised without religion by parents who were proud to have been raised the same way, Steiner was still Jewish enough to know that when he started to muse about the pleasures of a homogenous society, he was not only thinking ugly thoughts: he was acting against his own self-interest. Murray had taken care to remind Steiner of the appalling things people said about Jewish immigrants not that long ago, or indeed what established German Jews said about newly arrived Russian Jews, Jews just like Steiner's grandparents, to be more precise. "Even in *The New York Times*," Murray would lecture, "there were editorials denouncing Polish Jews and Russian Jews—your grandparents!"

"Gilles, you are a better person than I am," Steiner said.

"I am better at Ping-Pong, that we know for sure," Gilles concluded, and he opened the door to the kitchen where his friend Pierre, dressed in the same sort of barn coat that Gilles had worn in town, stood by the large, wood-burning stove with a bushel of oysters in his arms, and three loaves of *pain de campagne* from Poilâne under his arm.

The opening of the oysters seemed to be a ritual that Gilles and Pierre traditionally performed together, so Steiner asked Mary—and anyone else who wanted to—to join him for a walk. Mary was the only taker.

"Bread from Poilâne," Steiner told Pierre before heading out. "It's my favorite bakery in Paris."

"It is everyone's favorite," Pierre said in only slightly accented English. "I prefer Eric Kayser, on rue Monge, but it was closed. So…."

Steiner and Mary began their solitary walk along the twisting, muddy dirt road that ran past Gilles' house and headed down through a small valley. As per Gilles' instructions, they kept bearing left, past the large homes of the well-to-do Parisians who were just discovering this area, past the farms where a few goats grazed among the horses, and on up into the collection of a dozen or so small two-story homes grouped together at the top of a low hill. The grass was surprisingly green for this time of year. Gilles had said that the area was always rainy, which perhaps explained the phenomenon. They walked for half an hour before turning back to retrace their steps. Along the road, a small boy played with his Christmas present, a remote-controlled toy airplane. When he saw Mary and Steiner approaching, the boy turned towards his father and hid his head in the man's belly.

On the road heading back to Gilles' house, Mary tried to call Michael on her cell phone, but there was no answer. So this became not only the first Christmas they'd spent without their only child; they hadn't even managed to speak with him on the phone. Well, Michael was no doubt glad to have his parents an ocean away over the Christmas break.

Up ahead young life presented itself: there was Catherine who was taking her little brother Michel for a walk.

"Papa said to come to find you," Catherine said. "He thought you might be lonely."

"Your father is a considerate man," Steiner said.

"He has manners, dear," Mary told her husband in a way that Steiner experienced as suggesting somehow that he himself had none.

"Dinner is almost ready," the girl said.

Catherine looked just like her mother: high cheekbones, blue-gray eyes, clear skin. Lucky girl, Steiner thought. Given the choice between being too beautiful or not sufficiently beautiful, Catherine definitely bore the more desirable burden.

As the foursome turned to walk back to the house, little Michel ran ahead and then turned to run back, laughing with glee in his tiny brown wool jacket and bright blue miniature Nike shoes. Catherine leaned down as Michel reached her, lifted her brother into the air, and gave him a kiss on the cheek. If that is not love, Steiner thought, I don't know what love looks like.

"Ooh, la, la," Catherine said, and everyone laughed together.

As soon as Catherine put Michel back on the ground, the little boy ran a few steps down the road and then circled back to run at his sister, but instead of lifting the child again, Catherine spread her legs. Michel tucked his head down like a miniature halfback and ran between his sister's legs, laughing and smiling. Then he circled back to run down the road yet again. As Michel, screeching with delight, approached this time, Steiner spread his legs and Michel veered to run between them.

What possibly could be more pleasant than this moment? Yes, this was happiness, there was no other word for it. To be walking through a beautiful valley on Christmas day with the laughing children of an old friend who used to kick your ass at tennis and had just kicked it again at Ping-Pong, this was the thing itself, and Steiner, for once, seemed to actually know it.

Steiner, though, found himself remembering the day his own Michael, then a boy of only eight or nine, was playing with his Little League team in Central Park. Michael, who wasn't much of an athlete, was always stuck playing right field and rarely got a hit. On this day, Michael had reached first base after being hit by a pitch. When the next boy at bat smacked the ball into the outfield, Michael quickly ran to third base, but then, without looking up, he ran towards home plate, though everyone could see Michael would be called out.

"Slide!" Steiner shouted, "Slide."

But Michael didn't slide. Not that it would have mattered: he was, as they say, out by a mile.

"Why didn't you slide?" Steiner asked as his son returned to the bench. And then Michael kicked his father in the left shin with all the force the boy could muster. Which was quite a bit of force, very impressive for such a little kid.

"Son of a bitch," Steiner said, "son of a bitch," an interesting choice of words in retrospect.

Back at Gilles' house, normal life, family life, and Christmas Day itself all continued to move forward. As scheduled, Pierre's wife Deborah had just arrived from Paris with their daughter who was the same age as Catherine. Deborah, an American lawyer, was pretty in a New

England sort of way, and Steiner despaired of ever eyeing an unattractive human being again. Perhaps he'd have to wait until he returned to New York, or at least until he gave himself a careful inspection in the bathroom mirror. Deborah was straightforward and friendly in ways that her husband Pierre didn't seem to be. She wore her hair in a ponytail, but somehow managed an air of sophistication in simple slacks, green sweater, and scarf tied deftly around her neck. The couple had a house nearby, but lived in the Marais.

"What a beautiful jacket," Jean told Mary, as she and Steiner took off their outdoor layers.

"I got it yesterday," Mary reported.

"At Lagerfeld Gallery," Steiner said.

"Well, I'm quite jealous," Jean said with that Dublin accent that struck Steiner as insincere when Steiner first met her years ago, though he now realized it was just the way Jean talked.

"I saw Lagerfeld last night," Deborah said.

"No! Really?" Steiner said.

"It is not so strange to see Karl Lagerfeld," Pierre said.

"I took my daughter to Midnight Mass at Notre Dame," Deborah said. "We drove out here this morning. It felt like all of Paris was jammed into the cathedral last night. Just before it started, we heard a noise from the back of the church. Everyone turned around to see who it was. And it was Lagerfeld with two of the most beautiful young men you've ever seen."

"Of course," Pierre said.

"There's no doubt it was him with the white ponytail and the sunglasses. Very striking."

"He's so skinny now," Steiner said, and it struck him as odd that six adults were standing in a beautiful house on Christmas Day speaking with excitement about the sight of a fashion designer in a church.

"I met Lagerfeld at a luncheon last year," Jean said. "It was arranged by French *Vogue*. I'd written a piece for them. He's a very brilliant man. He didn't eat his food; he just pushed it around his plate. But he's very charming, very curious. He was taking tango lessons and learning how to be a bartender. He speaks several languages, and seems to be interested in everything. He was born quite rich, you know, but he works very hard. He owns houses all over the world."

"That's rich," Steiner said.

"He sent me an invitation to a Chanel ready-to-wear show, but I couldn't go," Jean said.

"Oh you should have gone," Deborah said. "I would have gone with you."

"This is turning into a Karl Lagerfeld Christmas," Steiner said. "I barely knew who the guy was until last week. But I still don't care about Karl Lagerfeld, and he doesn't care about me."

"What do you think of that diet book he wrote?" Mary asked Gilles, ignoring Steiner's comment and perhaps displeased with it. "You're the expert."

"It is silly," Gilles said with a shrug. "You should eat your food, not push it around the plate."

"But you haven't read the book, dear," Jean said.

"There is only one way to lose weight," Gilles said. "Eat less and exercise more. That is my diet book. One sentence. But I will never sell a million copies, I don't think, like Jean's books."

"I've never sold a million copies," Jean said.

"Yes, but you come close enough to buy this house," Gilles said with an air of contentment. "So for me it is the same thing."

Steiner and Pierre stood in the barn of a living room where they'd been sent to set the table.

"Gilles tells me you're an economist," Steiner said to fill the silence.

"Yes," was all that Pierre said in reply.

Steiner decided to say nothing until spoken to. He noticed with some pleasure that beneath Pierre's heather-colored cashmere sweater lurked a small gourmand's gut, just like Gilles'. Perhaps the Lagerfeld diet was in order. But Pierre was a tall guy, so the belly didn't much matter. Mary had once told Steiner that he didn't understand anything about what women find attractive in men. To Steiner, ignorance in this case did not seem like a significant shortcoming in a husband.

After another ponderous minute of absolute quiet, Steiner gave in. Feeling like a dog who turns over on its back to show submission,

Steiner said, "Why don't you make one place-setting and I'll just copy what you do."

"That will be fine," Pierre said, and he slowly set a place at the head of the long table that almost ran the length of the dining room.

Ten chairs were arranged around the table, four on each side, and two places at either end. The sound of the children's movie bled into the air from the next room.

Pierre arranged the unmatched, somehow delicate-looking plates, napkins, forks, spoons, and knives exactly as Steiner would have, except that he placed a fish knife and a small fork above the place. Steiner imagined that Jean had collected the mix of plates and cutlery at local shops over the years. There was something messily elegant about the way they came together on the table.

"Gilles told me you worked in California for a while," Steiner said, trying to fill the air with conversation like a host on a talk show with a guest who just doesn't want to talk.

"Yes," Pierre said, "I was in Brentwood, where O. J. Simpson kill his wife. And before that I was in New York."

It was beginning to amuse Steiner to see just how cold Pierre could be.

"Is that how you met your wife – in America?" Steiner asked.

"Yes, in Los Angeles," Pierre said.

Now is the part of the conversation where you're supposed to ask me a question, Steiner thought, as he laid out more place settings. Steiner was working more quickly than Pierre, but not doing as good a job: Pierre's settings were much straighter. Steiner never could really concentrate on things like place settings: that's what prop people were for. He circled back to the three places he'd already set, and tried to make them neater.

"You are doing very well," Pierre said.

"Thank you. How long have you known Gilles?"

"I went to school with his brother Olivier. What you call high school."

"Olivier is doing very well."

"Yes."

This clearly was the worst five minutes so far of Steiner's trip to France. It was more immediately unpleasant than getting fired from his old job. On the day that he was laid off, Steiner at least knew exactly what he was supposed to do and say.

"So what do you do in Paris?" Pierre asked finally.

"What do I do?" Steiner said. Though he understood the question, he wanted Pierre to imagine that his English was unintelligible.

"With your time. With your day. How do you pass the time?"

"Walking around, looking at the city. Shopping. I like to go shopping."

"Shopping, yes," Pierre said, and Steiner couldn't guess what that meant.

"And we go to museums, of course," Steiner said. "Yesterday we went to the Balzac museum."

"Balzac?"

"Yes, in Passy. The Maison de Balzac. It's a tiny museum in the old house where Balzac lived towards the end of his life. We go there every time we're in Paris. It's a kind of pilgrimage."

"But you have so many other museums, of course."

"My wife and I have been reading all of Balzac's work we can find in English," Steiner offered, knowing that he was exercising a wrong-headed impulse to expose something he loved to someone he already pretty much hated. "Do you read Balzac?" Steiner asked. "Do people read him in France today?"

"Not so much anymore," Pierre said. "My grandmother, yes, she read Balzac. But you have to read French to know what a difficult writer he is. He is not pleasant. The way he admires so much the aristocrats...the sentimental stories...it is all so old-fashioned. The criminals. He is fascinated with criminals—like an American. The characters are not characters, they are types or monsters. And he has each time the same plot. Always about money, always about greed. The same story each time. When you start, you know already what will be the end. Every novel is the same, no? I advise you to stop wasting your time."

They had finally finished setting the table, and Steiner was entirely without words. For the second time this week, he felt like he might never speak again.

"It is good," Pierre said, looking over the table.

And he was right. Winter light poured in from the windows. The mix of floral patterns in the table cloth, napkins, and plates—all the blue, pink, yellow, and purple flowers that Steiner could not name—somehow made him feel optimistic.

"Where do you stay in Paris?" Pierre asked, buoyed by either the completion of a job well done, or his quick—and unanswered—demolition of Steiner's literary hero.

Steiner explained, at too great length he instantly regretted, that he'd lost his job and had been offered the apartment of friends who were covering the coming war.

"We were just here in the spring," Steiner said. "But we couldn't resist coming back. It's such a great apartment. So far this war is working out well for us."

"Yes," Pierre said, "so far the American army has succeeded in killing one French cameraman."

"I read about that," Steiner said. "Terrible."

"And the war has given you a nice holiday. Very good. Your country is to be congratulated."

The oysters and foie gras, together with the champagne and mysteriously wonderful Alsatian white that went along with it, was dinner enough for Steiner, but this was a nineteenth-century-style feast, or so it felt to him, and Steiner knew it was his duty to soldier on. Gilles and Jean were at the heads of the table, and Steiner was seated at Jean's right, where he felt oddly safe. When a beautiful woman wants to make you feel at home, she gets the job done. Pierre was across from Steiner, with Mary on his left. Gilles was at the opposite end of the table with Pierre's wife and all the kids. If his presence was intended to keep order, it was certainly succeeding: the children were as quiet at the dinner table as Steiner remembered having been when he was a kid and unfamiliar adults came over for a meal.

Pierre had brought the two loaves of foie gras—each the size of the carrot bread that Mary sometimes baked in the country—and Pierre took credit for making it, though what exactly that entailed, Steiner wasn't sure. Had Pierre force-fed the geese? Had he slaughtered them? One of the loaves of foie gras—easily the freshest Steiner had ever

113

tasted—was mixed with morels, and the other was combined with papaya, of all things. Steiner guessed that Pierre's creative contribution consisted of mixing the foie gras with the other ingredients. The papaya was sort of an interesting idea, he had to admit, though it sounded stupid when Pierre first mentioned it.

At Steiner's end of the table, the topic of conversation was precisely the thing he wished to avoid: the impending war in Iraq. As soon as Pierre had made the crack about the French cameraman, Steiner sensed he'd be taking shit about it all night. What was he supposed to do? Mary was saying that America was not, in her view, truly a participatory democracy because there was no draft.

"If rich people's children had to fight, we wouldn't be going in there so quickly," she said. "Only two or three members of Congress have a child in the military. In America, rich people's kids usually don't join the army."

"What about in France?" Steiner asked. "Isn't there a draft?"

"There was until recently, but now it is no more," Gilles said.

"Well, what about you?" Steiner asked Gilles. "You weren't in the army, were you?"

"No, I make an excuse and they let me out."

"It was very easy to get out of it," Pierre said.

Gilles looked at Pierre and asked, "Were you in the army?"

"No, no," Pierre said, without offering any information about how he avoided it.

Curious that the two old friends had never discussed the topic before.

"So who goes in the army?" Steiner asked.

"You know, like the boy here in this village who make repairs on the house," Pierre said. "What is his name, Gilles?"

"Marcel," Jean said.

"Yes," Pierre said. "He grow up here in this small town. He goes in the army. It is his only time he leave his home. It is good for him. He is young. He sees a bit of the world. Then he comes back and he lives here in the village. That is who goes in the army in France"

"Don't some of the kids from around here go to Paris?" Steiner asked.

"Maybe one or two, but no, typically not," Pierre said. "You ask the farmer next door to me—the man who give me the foie gras—or the man who has the bakery in the village, the last time he was in Paris. He will say maybe ten years ago. Maybe he go to Paris to a doctor if he is sick. Or bring his mamma to see Gilles and ask why she is so fat. But that is all. You go more than one half-hour from Paris, and most ordinary people—they never go to the city. This is normal."

"It's not like that in America," Steiner said.

"Trust me," Pierre said. "I know. I spend three years in New York. You go to Connecticut, an hour outside of New York, and the people there, they know nothing about New York."

Look, Steiner wanted to say. I lived my whole fucking life in New York, and I have a house in Connecticut, and you don't know what you're talking about. But the weight and conviction of Pierre's snobbery paralyzed Steiner: he just wasn't expecting it, and now there was nothing Steiner could do. He was blindsided.

"Pierre, please," Gilles said finally, "you cannot lecture my friend about a city where he has lived his whole life. It is Christmas. We are having dinner. You are my guests."

"May we leave the table?" Catherine asked.

"But we haven't eaten our turkey," Jean said brightly. "It's Christmas; we must eat our turkey and pudding."

Once the turkey had been served, Mary drifted into conversation with Pierre's wife and Jean about the television version of one of Mary's books which had just aired on French TV. Please don't ask me if I've read the book, Steiner thought as he watched Pierre dissect his turkey wing with delicacy while keeping a close eye on his daughter, whom he had warned not to drink too much wine

How much booze had Steiner himself downed? There was the glass of champagne. No, it was two glasses. The Alsatian white that Steiner praised so much that Gilles re-filled his glass. And this was his second glass of Beaune. No, it was the third glass, and it was really more like a half glass. But despite all the alcohol, Pierre's chilliness oppressed Steiner. Some people just have the whammy on you. That was a line from *Something Happened*, the novel that helped Steiner understand his father. And Steiner felt more like Murray's son than usual at the moment: he felt like an unsubtle provincial from the Upper West Side, as Gilles and Pierre chatted quietly in French. They were talking about the food.

"Be careful," Jean told Pierre. "Mr. Steiner over here speaks French very well."

That was a bit of lie, but Steiner was grateful to Jean for saying it. Jean was an expatriate, an Irish woman living in France, so she had an abiding sympathy for anyone who wasn't a member of the club, no matter which club it was. This is why she was being kind to Steiner, he thought. Perhaps she also had come to like Steiner over the years of politely tolerating the company of this American who shared a bond with her husband. And while Steiner might be a depressive, there wasn't much to dislike in the unassuming, eager-to-please—and therefore somewhat boring—version of himself he presented in Paris during his annual visits.

"Is it me," Steiner asked Gilles, "or is Paris more expensive than it used to be? I usually never notice these things, but the meals seem to cost the same as in New York. And clothing too. A few years ago, everything was cheaper. Maybe even last year. But not now."

This wasn't really the right material, Steiner knew, but it was all he had.

"It's your dollar," Jean said. "It's not as strong as it was last year."

"Yes, yes, of course you're right," Steiner said.

"And the Euro is strong," Gilles said.

"It is simple," Pierre told Steiner. "Now you know how we feel here in Europe. Finally, you have 9/11, you have the wars, you have a small depression with your economy, you lose your job, and you can't believe it. Suddenly, your dollar is not so strong. Americans today are like children who leave home for the first time. You were rich and now you are not so rich. You yourself probably will never have another job as good as the one you just lost where you will win as much money. This is history. This is economics. This is what happens. Believe me. I am an economist, and I understand these things. You are finally learning about normal life."

⁑ SEVEN ⁑

Christmastime in Paris was turning into what people hoped for from April in Paris: mild temperatures, the threat of rain that never materializes in earnest, and then triumphant sunshine. Steiner and Mary were headed for a final walk to the Seine. Later they would figure out where to eat on this night when most restaurants in Paris were boarded shut.

This was Saint Stephen's Day, as Mary reminded Steiner, almost twenty-four hours since the mammoth Christmas Day feast in Burgundy, and Gilles' expert medical prediction was proving to be correct: Steiner felt like he might not eat again for a week. Why had he eaten the cheese course? Why had he followed up with so much of Jean's delicious Christmas pudding? To soak up all the booze, probably. No real hangover, though. Maybe Mary was right: good wine doesn't really fuck you up.

Steiner had run in the Tuilleries early that morning, happily sweating his ass off in the spring-like sun that burned through the winter gloom as the sun rose. When he returned from his run and walked into the entranceway of Tad and Judith's apartment building, he realized that he'd had yet another nostalgic Parisian experience: he'd stepped in dog shit, just like he'd done two or three times a week back in his student days when the citizens of Paris had no laws to ignore about cleaning up after one's pet. Steiner returned quickly to the street and tried all his old tricks: he scraped his shoe on the sidewalk, stepped into a puddle, and used a stick to clean between the grids which the manufacturers of athletic shoes seemed to have designed to make the removal of dog shit all but impossible. Steiner's efforts were fifty percent successful by the time he took off the offending shoe before walking back into the apartment.

117

"You got most of it," Mary said. "Let's just deal with it in New York." This was fine with Steiner, who watched gratefully as Mary, with female efficiency, wrapped the shoe in a plastic bag and then another, thicker plastic bag. One good thing about growing up in the country like Mary was that animal excrement was never a big deal to her like it was to city folk: it was just part of normal life. Besides, she loved dogs, and to complain about anything they did seemed morally incorrect in her somewhat Arcadian worldview.

Mary advised Steiner not to let the dog shit—or the shit Steiner had taken from Pierre—ruin the couple's last hours in Paris. They spent much of the day walking around the great city with their jackets tied around their waists, once again happy to be where they were. They surrendered to the absurd sentimentality of their trip: they had come to Paris to lose themselves and renew themselves. Well, why the fuck not? What harm would it do?

Steiner had to admit, however, that he *was* quite fucked up by his encounter with Pierre—if it was an encounter. But that suggested somehow that Steiner had defended himself, and he realized that he hadn't. Still, Steiner had to agree with what Mary said on the train ride back to Paris: "Pierre really did make a few good points." Which is what Steiner told Gilles after Gilles called to apologize for Pierre's behavior. "Pierre is very angry about this war," Gilles said. "It is not normal for him to be like that. Please forgive him."

But Pierre was right, Steiner thought: Steiner's fate was being decided by history in ways he was only beginning to understand. Well, it's hard to figure out what's happening to you while it's happening. But clearly history was now this thing out there that might take away Steiner's career, his summer house, his co-op apartment, his pride, his power to purchase really great clothes. History was this force that seemed suddenly to be intruding on his plans. History could even kill him, as surely as the Nazi soldiers who shot at his own father could have killed Murray.

Compared to Murray, though, Steiner felt he was experiencing a light version of history—just like all the supposedly light food that was marketed with such success to Steiner's fellow Americans who managed to stay fat anyway. The recession that came after 9/11 was nothing compared to the Great Depression, and Steiner expected to safely watch the coming war in Iraq on TV as he sat in the comfort of either his apartment in New York or his place in the country. The attacks of 9/11 killed more Americans than Pearl Harbor, but the wars that followed were unlikely to kill as many as World War II which, Steiner once read, took 60 million lives. Sixty million.

Steiner had lost his job, but so what? He had money in the bank, and he'd get another job. Beneath all his gloom, he was an optimistic American who'd been beaten up a bit by a snotty Frenchman. Yet his week in Paris with Mary was almost over, but what had Steiner accomplished? He'd been a mere consumer. He'd looked again at the familiar paintings at the Musée d'Orsay and felt surprised that the pigment on the canvases hadn't been worn away by all the admiring eyes that had passed over them. He'd taken in the Matisse and Picasso exhibit at the Grand Palais, though nothing about the paintings seduced him, invited him into their world. This was Steiner's fault, he knew, not Pablo's and certainly not Henri's. He bought Mary that jacket; he got himself a sweater and the knee-high Argyle socks he loved from Bon Marché. And Mary had treated herself to a new weekend bag at Louis Vuitton.

"I love the leather," Mary said with unashamed enthusiasm at the store next to Les Deux Magots. "It's sort of pebbly, and it's not quite black. It's grayish black. Plus, it doesn't have one of those awful LV logos on it. It's perfect."

Pierre was correct: these days the bag probably cost just as much in Paris as it did on Fifth Avenue, but Mary wanted it anyway, so she plopped down the green Amex card she refused to exchange for any of the fancier ones she was offered. The salesman was Japanese and his English was very weak. French was his second language, so he spoke slowly enough that Steiner was able to understand every single word he said. There they were, a gay 23-year-old from the suburbs of Tokyo and a forty-nine-year-old unemployed Jew from West End Avenue whose wife was overpaying for a French valise. They chatted about the changes in Saint-Germain-des-Prés over the years. No, Steiner told the young man, the Vuitton shop had never been a bookstore. The bookstore in question was called Le Divan, and it used to be across the way— where Dior is now.

The whole experience of buying the bag was an extremely pleasant, modern international capitalist ritual mixing money, flattery, and narcissism. This is the global economy in action, Steiner thought, his interior monologue echoing half-understood rhetoric from the business section of the *Times*.

So yes, Steiner had shopped a great deal in Paris. What else had he done? He'd walked through the Mouffetard market and thought, as he always did: Doesn't that fish look fresh? Isn't the beef redder here than in New York? He'd consumed wine, coffee, and too much food; he'd caught up with old friends, and had his feelings hurt by strangers. It had not exactly been eventful. If Fitzgerald was correct and character was action, Steiner was in big trouble: he'd done almost nothing. But if shopping was character, then Steiner was a Hemingway hero.

"Hey, hey, over here."

Steiner heard the voice as he and Mary walked hand-in-hand up towards the Seine on the Rue de Buci at twilight. It was an American's voice, the voice of an American man. Instinctively, Steiner ignored it, pretending he didn't hear.

Madame Vatel always called this street "*l'estomach de Paris,*" Paris' stomach. There were more bakeries back then, but even now the merchants still set out stands on the street. Butchers, cheese sellers, the old women who sold fruit—they all seemed to be in place when Steiner walked by here the other morning. Now with the shops closed on the day after Christmas, Steiner could see that the street hadn't really changed all that much. But so what if it had? Why shouldn't it change? Steiner certainly had.

"Aren't you going to come and say hello?"

It was them.

"We're trapped," Mary said.

Sitting at the café tables facing the street beneath the red and white candy-striped awnings of the Bar du Marché were Jim and Buzz, together again, their ruined faces and stained denim looking no worse than they did the other night. He'd bet that they were pretty drunk by now. After all, it was almost six at night.

"I'm buying," Jim said, as he stood to kiss Mary on both cheeks. "To make up for that awful meal on the Île."

Buzz shook Steiner's hand and smiled a pleasant enough smile.

"It wasn't that bad," Steiner said.

"Don't lie to me," Jim said.

"Yes, darling, don't lie," Mary added.

Suddenly—and briefly—it felt like they were all friends.

Jim and Buzz had both emptied their enormous glasses of Carlsberg. Beer seemed liked a fine idea, so Steiner ordered one, while Mary asked for a Kir.

"That's a very girlie drink," Buzz said.

"I'm a girl," Mary answered quickly.

"Well, what have you been up to since we saw you last?" Jim asked, looking at Mary.

"Shopping," Mary said.

"Where? What did you buy?"

"Do you really care?" Mary said.

"We're representatives of the Paris tourist board," Buzz said. "We're doing research on how tourists spend their money. We have to file a report."

For a moment Steiner considered reviving an expression from his childhood: Do you want to make something of it? He really wasn't in the mood to be fucked with. He'd had just about enough of that.

"Look, do we have to talk about this right now?" Steiner asked.

"No, no, no," Buzz said. He turned to Mary, "Tell me what do you do for a living. I don't think you ever told me."

"Yes I did. I run an independent press in New York. I'm a publisher."

"What kind of books do you publish?"

"She's not going to publish your memoirs," Jim told Buzz.

"I'm not going to write them," Buzz said. "I'm a TV producer. I can't write."

"I didn't even know you could read," Jim said.

The doors to the café were still open, despite the increasing chill. Steiner remembered coming to this bar with Gitta years ago. It was all but unchanged, as crowded as ever, and the acrobatic waiters with their drink-filled trays seemed oddly familiar. Even their faces felt familiar,

121

as if these were the sons of the men who'd worked here years ago. The ugly mosaic floor, the brown Formica tables, the cacophony of French dialogue, it all made Steiner happy, as did the sight of the drinks arriving. This was a wonderfully unimproved place.

"To Judith," Steiner said, lifting his beer.

"To her safe journey," Mary said.

All drank in silence, as if contemplating what Judith might be doing at the moment in Baghdad and what Buzz himself would be doing quite soon, too.

"So what kind of books do you publish?" Buzz asked Mary again.

"You probably never heard of them," Mary said.

"Try me. I love to read."

Mary mentioned her most widely known recent book— the one written in response to 9/11.

"Never heard of it,' Buzz said.

"It was on the cover of *Le Monde*," Steiner said proudly. "It's a best seller in France."

"I live in New York," Buzz said. "I read the *New York Post* and I subscribe to the *International Herald Tribune*—it's better than the *Times* because it doesn't have all that extra crap in it. But I read the classics."

"You do not," Jim said. "You are so full of shit."

"Try me," Buzz said.

"Who's your favorite author?" Mary asked.

"Honoré de Balzac."

"You are so full of shit," Jim said.

"Tell the truth and no one believes you."

"What Balzac character was a painter who grew up on the rue Mazarine near the Écoles des Beaux Arts?" Steiner asked, looking in the direction of the school he'd just mentioned.

"Let me see," Buzz said, pausing in what appeared to be genuine reflection.

"You are so full of shit," Jim said again.

"Joseph Bridau," Buzz said, "in *The Black Sheep*. Later in the novel he has a studio right over here on the rue de Seine."

"You're right," Steiner said. "Amazing. Amazing. I'm stunned."

"It's one of Balzac's best," Buzz said.

"I rank it with *Cousin Pons*," Steiner said. "And maybe *Goriot*."

"No, *Goriot*'s in the top rank–along with *Lost Illusions*," Buzz said. "Those are the best ones."

"You guys sound like little boys talking about your baseball cards," Mary said.

"You are outrageous," Jim said. "Outrageous!"

"What's wrong with Balzac?" Buzz said. "I love everything about him except his anti-Semitism."

"I thought you were an anti-Semite," Jim told Buzz.

"My father was a Jew."

"I didn't think you had a father," Jim said.

"Yeah," Steiner said, "the depiction of the Jewish characters can be a problem. They're always obsessed with money."

"But so was Balzac," Buzz said.

"You're right," Steiner said.

"You see," Buzz told Jim "There are things about me that you don't know."

"Do you think," Mary asked, "that the reason Balzac caricatures the Jews so much—I mean part of it was the times he lived in, of course. I mean, he's no worse than Shakespeare in *The Merchant of Venice*. And if you look at Balzac's work, he doesn't really like anyone all that much, except maybe aristocrats and extremely devout innocents. But I mean, he's equally offensive to the Poles. And what is he accusing the Jews of? …Being obsessed with money. Which is what Balzac himself was, of course. Gobseck and Nucingen were just better at getting money than Balzac. I mean, Balzac tried to make money like they did, but he was a lousy businessman. I think it's really what Jungians call shadow…"

A cell phone rang and everyone at the table, except for the phone-less Steiner, reached for their cells. Across the crowded cafe, two waiters pulled out their phones and said, "Hallo? Hallo?"

The ringing continued and Mary took her cell from her purse, as she said, "That must be Michael."

"I have no idea what anyone is talking about," Jim said. "I never graduated from college."

"Neither did I," Buzz said. "I dropped out after two years and went right to work as a copy boy."

"Hello darling, it's you, " Mary said, nodding and smiling at her husband. "Hold on a second, dear."

"It's our son," Steiner said.

Mary, with her cell phone pressed to one ear and her finger stuck in the other, grabbed her Lagerfeld jacket off the back of her chair, and walked through the open door to the street. Maybe she's afraid that Buzz or Jim will steal the jacket, Steiner thought. Maybe she was right. Steiner stood to join his wife, making a point to politely excuse himself because he guessed it was something Buzz or Jim would never do.

Mary had walked a few steps away from the café. Steiner, wearing only a thin wool sweater over his jeans, was chilly in the night air. This was December, after all. Steiner never really knew what the temperature was in Paris because he still had trouble converting Celsius to Fahrenheit, or was it the other way around? Steiner hadn't learned in twenty-five years, and was unlikely to do so in however many years remained in his life.

"But you're all right, darling?" Mary said with serious female worry in her eyes. It was a far graver expression than Steiner had seen the day he told her he was going to lose his job.

"What? What?" he asked.

"Your son was arrested."

"Arrested?"

Steiner thought immediately of pot. God damn it, why hadn't Michael listened to what Steiner told him about not smoking in the park? What a huge pain in the ass this is going to be. Shit. Steiner felt like Michael had kicked him in the shin again. Maybe Murray could get someone from his old law firm to handle it. No, bad idea. Wait, years ago Steiner had produced a show with a famous criminal defense attorney in New York. He did a lot of drug cases. Steiner began to figure out how to reach the guy right away. What was his name again?

"At the peace demonstration," Mary said.

"No!"

"Yes."

"How fucking stupid. Let me talk to him."

"Well, it sounds like you're fine, darling," Mary told Michael. "Don't worry about anything."

Before giving Steiner the phone, Mary put her hand over the receiver and told her husband, "Don't tell him that what he did was stupid."

"But it was," Steiner said.

"You're wrong," Mary said. "Just listen to me."

Steiner nodded and took the phone. The first words out of his mouth were, "Are you okay?"

"I'm fine, dad. I was with my friends the whole time. I told mom. It was nothing."

Michael's voice was filled with energy. He sounded alive, particularly when compared to his father. Yet Steiner couldn't imagine Michael's scrawny young body in jail overnight, his pale thin frightened face among all the street thugs with muscles, tattoos, and very bad skin. Steiner put the image out of his mind. Back when Steiner was in high school, his best friend had been arrested at the May Day demonstration at the Pentagon. When the kid returned to school, he became a celebrity, a hero who finally got to go out with the best-looking girls in their class.

"Tell me what happened," Steiner said.

"I told mom. It was only for one night. I was with three of my friends. They held us all together."

"Where?"

"On Centre Street."

"No!" Steiner said. "You were in the Tombs?"

"They don't call it the Tombs anymore."

"Yes they do."

"No, they don't. I was there, Dad."

"Now you're bragging about being arrested?"

"I'm not bragging," Michael said.

Mary gave Steiner a look that said: don't break his balls now please.

"How did you get out?" Steiner asked.

"The school came and bailed us out the next day. They hired us all a lawyer."

"What for?"

"There's going to be a hearing. The lawyer says the charges will probably be dismissed."

"What were the charges?"

"Disorderly conduct. We sat down when the cops told us to move."

125

Steiner didn't cherish the notion of his son giving cops a hard time. Didn't the police have better things to do than arrest children of privilege indulging in civil disobedience—or, worse yet, merely acting out, as the psychologists insisted on saying? Well, Michael was just exercising a fundamental American right, but when it came to cops, Steiner was as much of an establishmentarian as his own father. Cops had a very tough gig: their job was to deal with every asshole in New York who Steiner didn't want to deal with. And it was a big job, too, because there really was a steady supply of dangerous assholes out there. Why was his son adding to the cops' burden?

Mary gestured for the phone and mouthed a message to her husband: "Tell him you love him."

"We love you Michael," Steiner said. "You know that. Don't worry about this."

"Tell him you're proud of him," Mary said very quietly.

"I'm giving you to your mother," Steiner said instead.

Well, everyone in the world was having an adventure except for Steiner, he thought as he wandered away to give Mary a bit of privacy. No one likes to be listened to when they're on the phone—at least Steiner knew that he didn't like it.

When Steiner visited the Île de la Cité with Michael, the jail cells beneath it had fascinated the boy. Now Michael had done some time himself, just like Balzac's stint for evading the draft. Or was Honoré in for unpaid debt? Balzac had had his food catered while he was behind bars, and he'd entertained visitors in the private cell that was available to any prisoner with enough cash to pay for it. It must have been like the first-class cars they used to have in the Paris Metro: they weren't great, but they were slightly better than what everyone else was stuck with.

Perhaps Mary was right: Steiner should have told Michael that his father was proud of him. But it seemed so sentimental. Besides, Steiner didn't want to lie, and he thought that what Michael had done was pointless, would do nothing to stop the war. It was mere self-expression, done largely so that Michael and his friends could star in a small-scale historical melodrama of their own making. What if they'd been raped or robbed in jail? What if he and his friends had been beaten up? Was this the way to stop the war? Of course, it was more than Steiner himself had done. And it was better than getting busted for smoking a joint in Central Park with your high school friends. It was a part of being young.

Just a few months earlier, Steiner and Mary had driven Michael up to college for the first time. Mary, with tears in her bright green eyes, headed back to the car after they'd said their good-byes. Steiner turned to follow, but then he could not help but look back. Michael had stopped in his path and turned, too, clinging to the moment just like his father. Michael's face was—what? He looked scared, and he looked, to Steiner at least, just like he did when he was six years old. It was as if Michael hadn't changed since the time he fell off his bicycle and gashed open his knee while going down the hill behind the Metropolitan Museum of Art in Central Park. Steiner had held his son's hand at Lenox Hill hospital while Michael received the first five stitches of his young life. Michael had that same scared expression on his face the day he started high school. And again when, during his senior year, Steiner had the distinct impression that Michael was going off to get laid for the first time.

Steiner knew Michael's expression all too well: he'd seen it in the mirror. Steiner was scared like that when he went off to college, and also when he arrived in Paris to begin his junior year. *That* scared him? Arriving in Paris in 1975 weighed down by too much luggage and a portable Smith Corona typewriter? It wasn't exactly war-torn Baghdad. What was there to be afraid of?

What a horrible thing to pass on to one's son—fear. Where did Steiner himself pick it up? Not from Murray, who relished a good fight with other lawyers, the guy behind the deli counter, anyone who'd play along. It must have been from Steiner's mother whose performing self, the one she had presented on TV, disappeared later in life. Once Lola was off the air, she felt invisible. She stayed at home too much and came to be afraid of the world, afraid that she'd fail again in her career, or slip on the ice on the way to buy bread at Zabar's on a winter afternoon. Or perhaps the fear was Steiner's own invention, a weakness that he'd unwittingly taught his son through the well-known process of mimesis.

But Michael had nothing really to be afraid of that day as he headed off to his freshman year at that precious college with its privileged kids who would turn out to be not quite as talented as they imagined themselves to be. Michael's pain would likely be confined to failing a course or discovering that a girl prefers sleeping with another boy who seems more handsome and confident. No, Steiner had wanted to tell his son, it is not pain that awaits you. It's just normal life, but it sometimes scares you just like it scared me.

That first day at college, Michael gave his father a shy wave, and Steiner responded with what he hoped was a manly smile. When their eyes met, father and son were both trying not to cry. They both succeeded, which was fine with Steiner. But by the time Steiner arrived back in the city, he could not shake the irrational feeling that he'd done something violent, somehow hurt his son. The day felt brutal, though it surely was not.

Now Michael had gone off, gone off bravely and gotten himself arrested protesting a war that Steiner—and just about everyone else he knew—thought was wrong. Good for Michael. Steiner was pleased to imagine that Michael was overcoming his fear. He'd been arrested, but so what? Maybe Steiner was wrong to judge so quickly. Well, he was wrong about everything else; why should this be any different? Perhaps Steiner should have listened to Mary and told Michael he was proud. But Steiner just didn't like to be told what to do.

Steiner stood on the corner of the rue de l'Echaudé and the rue de Seine with his eyes fixed distractedly to the north where he could sense the presence of the Seine without quite seeing it. When Mary called his name, he didn't turn to greet her. She approached him from behind and put her arm in his. It really was getting cold out.

"It is beautiful here, isn't it?" Mary said.

They walked back toward the café in silence. A slim man in tight-fitting clothes crossed the street and headed their way.

"Oh my goodness," Mary said. "It's Karl Lagerfeld."

And it was unmistakably him, an austerely elegant figure with dark glasses, thick gray hair pulled back into the well-known pony tail, tight flared jeans, fitted blazer with sharp tailored shoulders, narrow black tie, and a shirt with a high collar that would not have been out of place on a well-dressed gentlemen in the late nineteenth century. The designer seemed to look Mary up and down as he approached. His expression was severe but inscrutable behind the tinted lenses. Did he recognize

Mary's jacket as one of his own design, if indeed designers actually worked on the clothing that bore their name? Did the famous stranger bow slightly in Mary's direction? Perhaps.

"Bonsoir," Lagerfeld said in a clipped German accent, and then he walked on.

Well, that was certainly something. Steiner and Mary simply chuckled to themselves. Their mood brightened. They were definitely having a more amusing evening than their son.

Just before Steiner reached the café, Mary took his hand. If Buzz and Jim hadn't been watching them, Steiner would have tried to give his wife his best kiss. Both men stood as Mary and Steiner returned to the table.

"Such good manners," Mary said. "I'm impressed."

"Everything all right?" Buzz asked.

"Yes, everything's fine," Mary said, and Steiner thought: how smart not to share the news about Michael with these strangers.

"We just saw Karl Lagerfeld," Steiner couldn't help but report.

"He looks awful," Jim said. "I saw him at the Chanel show in the fall."

"Well, he looked great to me," Mary said. "I love Karl Lagerfeld."

"Our son was just arrested in New York," Steiner said, checking to see if Mary cared that he'd brought it up just to change the subject. She didn't seem to mind.

"What for?" Buzz asked, sounding very much like a journalist.

"He was at a peace demonstration," Mary explained. "The cops told him to move, but he and his friends refused. They're into civil obedience: they wanted to get arrested. So they spent a night in jail."

"Is he okay?" Jim said, suddenly a concerned neighbor in a small middle-American town. Maybe this is what his own parents were like.

"Oh he's fine," Mary said, turning to her husband. "He's fine, right dear?"

"He sounded great."

"Well good for him," Buzz said. "Listen, I've covered a lot of wars over the years, and I've never been in favor of one of them. You should be very proud of your son."

⚹ EIGHT ⚹

Nothing beats sitting next to a fit-looking giant of a Russian boy, no older than twenty-one and entirely paralyzed from the waist down, to take one's mind off the statistically miniscule threat of terrorism while crossing the Atlantic in a whale-sized Boeing 767. Or so Steiner thought as he contemplated the poor fellow on his right.

When the boy's father first pushed his son's wheelchair into the coach section of the plane, Steiner, like the majority of his fellow passengers, thought: Oh shit. Which is what most people think on a New York City bus when the driver commences the time-consuming chore of lowering the hydraulic lift that allows someone in a wheelchair to get on board. People groan because their time is being stolen. They groan because of the inestimable selfishness of our species. Inestimable is a word Steiner loved. He picked it up from John Cheever; stole it, really.

As soon as Steiner saw the Russian boy, he guessed that they'd wind up sitting next to each other. Plenty of others on the plane had had the same irrational premonition, no doubt, but only Steiner's proved correct. At first, Steiner thought the father and son were French, so he greeted them with a "Bonjour," which they returned easily enough. But the father wasn't French, and he became more and more frustrated as he tried to communicate with the Air France flight attendant in extremely broken French before switching to even worse English. When father and son spoke with the older gray-haired man in pee-stained khaki pants who'd been allowed to accompany them onto the plane to help the kid get seated, Steiner was all but certain that they were speaking in Russian.

The father's broad flushed Slavic face would have fit in quite easily about ten seats down from Brezhnev in a thirty-year-old photo of the

Kremlin bureaucracy. Dad looked like an official in the ministry of agriculture, an old Kruschev-era retainer. With the help of his older Russian friend, the father prepared to lift the crippled boy—his name was Dimitri, Steiner later discovered—into the aisle seat on Steiner's right, the very seat that Steiner himself had been hoping to steal later on in the flight.

"No, no, don't put him here," Mary said slowly and loudly while everyone on the plane, Steiner among them, instantly thought: what a selfish bitch.

"Be quiet," Steiner said.

"No, you don't understand," Mary said, which pissed Steiner off because he thought that lately Mary had been suggesting, more often than usual, that her husband was oddly unintelligent in certain areas such as spatial relations.

"Just let him sit down," Steiner told his wife.

"You're so stupid," Mary said.

"I'm not stupid," Steiner said.

"*Excusez-moi*," Mary said, raising her voice and leaning forward in her seat, trying to get the attention of the flight attendant. But everyone was ignoring Mary who seemed like an awful angry woman who was just increasing the suffering of the poor crippled boy who was already being dropped into the seat next to Steiner's.

At the moment, Mary might have made the list of most evil human beings in the world in the estimation of the other passengers on the plane. Let's see, Osama Bin Laden was first. Then came Saddam Hussein. Or maybe it was the other way around by now. Then came that American bitch who was raising her voice at the poor Russian cripple who just wanted to sit down next to her husband and fly across the Atlantic to the good old USA.

With his son fully installed next to Steiner, the father sat down on the aisle across from his son at the end of the five seats in cabin's center row.

"You should switch seats," Mary told the father. "The other is better for him."

"*This, this*—this is his seat," the father said, pointing to where his son sat impassively, no doubt feeling like shit. The father gave Mary an angry, uncomprehending look, while the son, who had even less

131

English, could only point mournfully towards his middle and say, "From here down—nothing. No move."

"Just let it go," Steiner told his wife.

"You didn't get my point," she said.

And then he did.

With the huge immobile Dimitri on the aisle to Steiner's right, neither Steiner, sitting in the middle seat, nor Mary in the window seat to Steiner's left, could get up without literally climbing over Dimitri, whose long, immobile legs were pressed up against the back of the seat in front of him. If, as Mary had tried repeatedly to explain to everyone who by then—as Gilles would put it—double-hated her, the father had sat next to Steiner, then Mary and Steiner would not have been trapped. The four people to Dimitri's right in the free-standing center row of seats could have exited to their right because everyone else seated in that row could *stand up*.

"I didn't get what you were saying until it was too late," Steiner told Mary as a sort of apology for sitting by guiltily and uncomprehendingly as Mary took a brave, unpopular, but highly rational stand while her faithless husband was embarrassed and secretly hated her just like all the other right-thinking people on board the plane.

"You see, you didn't understand what I was saying. I was right."

"This is not a metaphor," Steiner said.

"You better hope not."

Well, if things had worked out differently, Steiner wouldn't now, two hours into the flight, know that Dimitri had "cousin" in Cleveland where he "go to get operation." And Steiner wouldn't know that Cleveland "have NFL football" which Dimitri apparently liked to watch on TV. Nor would Steiner know how poor Dimitri—a heartbreakingly muscular giant with at least an eighteen-inch neck that would not have looked out of place on a football field—ended up in his current physical condition.

"Chechnya," Dimitri said simply, twenty minutes after takeoff, at which point Mary, Steiner loved her so, had tears in her eyes.

"Is all right," Dimitri said, reaching across Steiner to pat Mary's hand.

"I'm sorry," Mary said.

"Sorry, me too," Dimitri said, stoically, as his father gave Steiner a brave smile from across the aisle. He'd forgiven Mary. Perhaps he'd even understood what she was trying to tell everybody. They were all friends now.

Like his father, Dimitri had equipped himself with no reading material for the flight that took off just before noon and would occupy the entire afternoon. The boy held a CD player in his hand and was listening to Hip-Hop recordings. Steiner was armed with that day's *Herald Tribune, Le Figaro,* which is the only Parisian daily Air France offered, plus the Penguin edition of the Balzac novel whose title was translated as *A Murky Business.* In French it was—what? *Une Ténébreuse Affaire,* Steiner reminded himself when he turned to the first page of the yellowing book that he'd bought used on the Internet. He doubted he could pronounce the title correctly in French. It wasn't one of Balzac's best, Steiner thought, feeling like an old widow midway through a murder mystery by Gilles' wife.

From *Le Figaro,* Steiner learned that even right wing French papers were deeply skeptical about the coming American war in Iraq, and from watching Mary gracefully push herself up and hop over the immobile Dimitri, he learned that all that time in yoga class certainly had paid off for his very limber wife. Steiner himself had twice almost kicked the poor kid in the nuts while clumsily climbing over him during multiple trips to the bathroom, though Steiner wondered if a kick to the nuts would have caused Dimitri physical pain anyway. Poor Dimitri wouldn't get to the john once in over seven hours. He must be wearing a catheter, Steiner guessed, or maybe a diaper. Steiner's instant, utterly ignorant prognosis for Dimitri was that the operation he was to undergo in Cleveland would fail. But what did Steiner know about the spinal cord? What did he know about miraculous cures?

He knew very little indeed.

He wasn't even sure where Chechnya was. From his daily deep immersion in the *Times,* Steiner knew only that it had been part of the Soviet Union, and that Chechnya was where the Russian government was fighting against the guerilla-style rebel forces it hoped to convince the world were terrorists, just like the sons of bitches in the Middle East. But was Chechnya, say, north of Moscow or south? Steiner didn't know.

Some stories you follow carefully, some you don't. Steiner felt vaguely as if his ignorance had contributed to Dimitri's plight. But if retaining everything one read in the *Times* could alleviate suffering, then his own mother would have already been awarded the Nobel Peace Prize five times over: she remembered everything and tortured anyone who would listen with all the gruesome details.

When the plane got closer to New York and the flight attendant came around with the white customs cards, Steiner attempted to explain, first to Dimitri—and then to his father, that the forms were only for American citizens. But the father especially seemed frightened of any paperwork—which was probably a very logical outgrowth of having spent the bulk of his lifetime as a citizen of the Soviet police state.

"Don't put down too many things," Mary told Steiner when he started to write on his customs form.

"Oh come on," Steiner said.

"They haven't changed the laws in years," Mary said. "They still only let you claim $400 per household. That's it. The amount hasn't changed in twenty-five years. No adjustment for inflation. That's ridiculous. Who spends only $400 in Paris?"

"Most people."

"Nonsense. Nobody tells the truth on these things. Why do you always have to be such a good boy?"

"I like to tell the truth."

"Do you think Gilles always tells the truth? Does Pierre?"

Steiner wrote down the price of the sweater that he'd picked up on rue de Grenelle. He considered listing the socks from Bon Marché, but he thought it would piss off his wife. He threw in one of Mary's purchases, too, one of the black turtlenecks he hadn't even realized she'd bought until they packed together in the morning. That's it. Mary seemed to be writing a lot, but then she told Steiner, "I'm not declaring the jacket."

"Oh come on."

"I took the tags off. I've been wearing it around. It doesn't look new. How do they know where I got it?"

"Because Lagerfeld Gallery isn't available in America?" Steiner said.

"You think they know that?"

"I'm sure they spend their spare time reading *Vogue*."

"Do you know that you're absolutely out of your mind?" was Mary's reply.

When the plane finally landed, Mary and Steiner waited until everyone else had gotten off to make sure that Dimitri and his father would be okay. The airline sent two black women equipped with a wheelchair to help, but they couldn't get the giant Dimitri out of his seat. He really was a huge kid, easily over two hundred pounds. Dimitri's father flushed with anger and spoke loudly in Russian. It would be fair to call it yelling. Steiner guessed that Papa didn't think two women— much less two black women—were appropriate choices to help lift a huge ex-soldier into a wheelchair. The father had probably never seen black women in a professional situation, if indeed he'd ever seen a black person before in his life. He was probably a racist. What were the odds that he wouldn't be?

"I can help you if you let me help you," one of the black women told the father, but he didn't understand what she said.

Well, Dad would learn if he wanted to get along in America. He'd learn that you take help where you can get it. The flight attendant watched passively as the crisis built, but she wouldn't let Steiner try to help the father pick up his son, so finally he and Mary were pretty much asked to leave the plane. They grabbed their things with a huge, unspoken sense of relief, and wished Dimitri luck. Steiner doubted it would help. He doubted anything would.

Mary tried calling Michael twice as soon as they stepped off the plane, but there was no answer. Steiner couldn't wait to see him. What was the jail in Centre Street like, he wondered? Did Michael have to pee in front of all the criminals in a shared toilet in an overcrowded cell? Had he had to defecate? Had he been able to? That for Steiner would be one of the worst things about jail—the complete loss of privacy. Throw in the threat of physical violence and rape, the lack of freedom, plus the awful food, rodents, foul smells, and jail really didn't seem like the sort of place Steiner hoped Michael would make a habit of visiting.

"Hello folks," the open-faced custom's official said from behind the bulletproof plastic booth when Steiner and Mary presented their passports.

"What were you doing in Paris?" he asked.

That question again. The world was truly obsessed with this issue. But Steiner was ready with his answer. He was prepared. He'd written down his line on a cue card and stored it in his brain.

"We were tourists," he said.

"Welcome home," the man said.

"It's good to be home," Mary said.

The man read over their white customs cards and used a yellow highlighter to make a mark across Steiner's card.

Shit, Steiner thought.

Once they'd moved a few steps away, Mary asked, "What did that line mean?"

"I guess we'll find out," Steiner said, but he didn't feel good about the situation, not at all, and he wasn't surprised when the next official they encountered told them to stand in a different line than the other passengers once they'd retrieved all their luggage.

"Why us?" Mary asked, as a polished-looking couple with about five square feet of Vuitton luggage hustled by on their way home, followed by a family of very rich-looking suburbanites with big bright boxes from Chanel, Dior, Fendi, and all the rest. It was incongruous to see all those slick, shiny shopping bags piled up in the sort of carts you see in the supermarket. Steiner guessed the family was headed home to Westchester with enough unclaimed merchandise to clothe two international opera stars for a year.

Once Steiner and Mary arrived in the special area reserved for suspect types such as themselves, another official unsmilingly took their passports and white forms. His silver badge informed them that he was a customs inspector. He wore a holster and a gun. Steiner's small family had encountered more armed officers in the last few days than in the previous forty-nine years of Steiner's life. This guy's gun was an ominous automatic, a nine-millimeter just like the New York cops used. And cops in Paris, too, if Steiner remembered correctly.

"I'm going to have to open a few of your bags," the official said, as he stood behind a metal table that reminded Steiner of an examination table in a doctor's office or maybe a morgue.

"Fine," Mary said, but she was scared.

It didn't help that she looked like a million bucks in that Lagerfeld jacket that, ignoring her husband's advice, she had not declared on her white form. Nor did it help that she had another winter coat—the one he'd bought her a year ago at Helmut Lang—stuffed into the grayish-black leather Vuitton bag she'd also picked up in Paris. Well, there's a reason most left-wing publishers aren't such maniacs about designer clothes, Steiner thought: it just ends up biting you on your very stylish ass. But it *was* a stylish ass, and Steiner took pride in it, even in the middle of this absurd moment.

Steiner hadn't seen Mary scared like this—ever. The prospect of childbirth seemed not to frighten her all that much, though Steiner had told her it would have scared him. "That's because you don't have a womb," Mary said. Come to think of it, she was almost this upset once, in his experience, when she got a speeding ticket down in the Florida Keys. Southern cops scare East Coast sissies. What a couple of wimps they were. Scared shitless at the prospect of getting caught illegally bringing an overpriced black tweed Gallery Lagerfeld jacket into America. Oh this was so stupid. Where had Mary put the receipt? He had no idea.

Another official came by, and the first one handed over Steiner and Mary's passports. The second man studied the passports and then studied their faces hard. How complicated is it? Steiner thought. That's a fuckin' picture of me. I haven't changed that much in the three years since it was taken. When the picture was taken I was younger and I thought it looked like shit, but now I kind of like it. It captures my more youthful, more innocent self. Now I realize it's a great picture. That's what it's like to get old.

The second officer disappeared with the passports.

"Where is he taking those?" Mary asked.

"To be checked," the first guy said.

"Can I make a call on my cell phone?"

"Not until we're done here, ma'am."

"I want to call my son."

"Sorry, not until we're done."

"Are we under arrest?" Steiner asked.

The guy couldn't suppress a smirk.

137

"You're not under arrest," he said.

Steiner squinted at the man's nametag and saw that his name was Dimitri. But he looked like a Greek Dimitri, not a Russian one. What were the odds of meeting two guys named Dimitri in the same day? What were the odds of having your fucking luggage inspected when you come back to America after a short trip to Paris? What are the odds of three people from the same middle-class family breaking the law during Christmas week of the year 2002?

Dimitri II, as Steiner now thought of him, pointed to Mary's new Vuitton bag and asked her to put it on the table so he could open it. Shit. Had she declared that bag? Probably not. Her and her goddamned privileged left-wing *je m'en fouisme*. It really pissed Steiner off. She was just like that stupidly arrogant bastard Pierre. Privileged people always thought they could beat the system, but Steiner was the kind of guy who always got caught—the kind who always had to obey the rules. That's why he told his accountant to take no chances. That's why he never claimed even a tiny tax deduction he couldn't prove. That's why he always told the truth on these goddamned customs forms. He'd told Mary. He'd warned her. He knew what the fuck he was doing.

After Mary placed the Vuitton bag on top of the metal table, Dimitri put on his plastic rubber gloves, unzipped the bag, and began to slowly go through its contents. It all made Steiner think vaguely of an autopsy. Dimitri used two hands to unwind the ball into which Mary had carefully rolled her dark gray Helmut Lang winter coat. Was it cashmere? Steiner couldn't remember. Dimitri couldn't feel the fabric, anyway, through the condom-like gloves.

"I bought that in New York last season," Mary said.

Like Dimitri gives a shit that this coat that cost two of his weekly paychecks is from last season, Steiner thought. Dimitri's face was not unkind, and he seemed a bit chagrined to have to perform his job. Steiner found his manner entirely sympathetic. Dimitri was just doing his job, but he wasn't getting his rocks off: he didn't particularly enjoy doing it.

"What's this?" Dimitri asked Mary.

He was holding Steiner's double-wrapped, dog-shit-soiled running shoe—the one Mary had put in two layers of plastic.

"It's my running shoe," Steiner said. "I stepped in some dog dirt in the park. We wrapped it up so it wouldn't stink."

Smart not to say dog shit, Steiner thought. Smart not to risk offending anyone's sensibilities in the present situation.

"Can I open it?"

"Sure, but it's pretty disgusting," Mary said.

Dimitri considered opening the bag, but he finally put it aside. Steiner could only imagine the things Dimitri found in people's luggage every day. He wanted to ask about it. Perhaps later.

Dimitri continued to slowly, delicately peel away layers of sweaters, T-shirts, bras, and panties, passing over the sweater that Steiner knew to be the one Mary bought the other day. This was truly the closest encounter Steiner had ever had with anyone resembling a cop. It was pretty awful, he had to admit.

"And what's this?" Dimitri asked next.

He was holding up a slip of paper. It was a fucking receipt. It said Lagerfeld Gallery on it. Oh this was a tough case, but Dimitri had cracked it. Mary really was a fucking idiot.

"It's a receipt for this jacket," Mary said, 'fessing up like the good citizen she was when she wasn't filling out customs forms on airplanes.

"Did you declare it?" Dimitri asked politely. He probably went through this a dozen times a day. It wasn't a great way to earn a buck, and he truly took no pleasure in it. But his calm manner really did help. Dimitri was in no way an asshole.

"No," Mary said. "I didn't. My husband told me to, but it was me...."

Oh she was cute when she was scared. It made her look young—like a teenager. The poor thing. It had been a while since Steiner felt protective of his fierce wife. It had been about twenty years. But like Dimitri, he took no pleasure from her suffering.

"It doesn't matter," Dimitri said. "Is there anything else? Because now is the time to tell me about it."

Dimitri looked Steiner's way. Steiner looked over at Mary. Was this glance towards his wife a betrayal—a way for Steiner to put the blame on her? Well, she'd already denounced herself to the authorities, so Steiner didn't feel all that bad about it.

139

"That bag is new; I didn't claim it," Mary said, pointing to the open satchel in front of Dimitri.

"Anything else?"

"I claimed everything I bought," Steiner said.

Steiner guessed that Mary's interior monologue was likely directed at her husband at the moment, and that it went something like: "Shut the fuck up you sanctimonious bastard."

"There might have been a sweater, too," Mary said.

"Might have been?" Dimitri asked.

"It wasn't very expensive. Maybe a hundred bucks, a hundred and fifty…"

Wrong answer. Dimitri probably didn't think that was inexpensive.

"I'm going to have to write it all down," Dimitri said. "And don't leave anything out. Then I'll talk to my supervisor."

What were they going to do? Arrest them? Could they be arrested for this? That would be too much. Poor Michael would laugh his ass off once he bailed them out. Oh that would be truly hilarious in some awful sort of way.

Unlike Dimitri, his supervisor, a rather stylish redheaded woman with a gun, mascara, copper-colored lipstick, and hard brown eyes, was one cop whose libido—as Mary would phrase it—was definitely engaged by work. In her New York street cop way, she seemed to get off on scaring the crap out of upper-middle-class smugglers of Vuitton who were having their once-in-a-lifetime first-hand encounter with the Federal government. Her nametag said "Janice Goldwasser." A Jewish woman with a civil service job. Think of all of the relatives who were disappointed in her. Think what Janice's mother said when Janice foolishly halted her education. Think of the resentments all around. Steiner knew he was screwed. Janice was a woman who was born to smuggle crap into the country, not find it in other people's overpriced luggage.

"Did you read the statement on this card before you signed it?" Janice Goldwasser asked Steiner and Mary.

"Yes," Mary said.

"And were your answers to the questions truthful?"

"No, our answers were not truthful," Steiner said, because his impression was that the ritual in which he was presently engaged was similar to getting a speeding ticket. Just as your best bet was to tell the officer at the roadside, "Yes sir, I was speeding, I'm sorry," here you needed to humbly admit what a stupid lying piece of shit you were. It was the pound of psychic flesh the individual in the uniform must extract from the guilty party who will soon get to wear the clothes they were attempting to sneak into the United States of America.

"But it's not fair," Mary said. "Why did you stop us?"

"We'll give you an informational brochure that will answer all your questions once we're finished here," Janice said. "If you have any problem with the way you're being treated, there's a number you can call."

"See what else you find," Janice told Dimitri. Turning next to Mary, Janice said, "If you're over the $1,600 limit, we'll seize the items in question."

"Seize them?" Mary asked.

"Yes, Ma'am."

"What does that mean? You take them?"

"That's what 'seize' means, ma'am," Janice said, and then she looked at Steiner who, in his agitated state, imagined that Janice's angry expression was meant to say, "You should have married a Jewish girl instead of this angry-looking goyish wife of yours."

"I thought the limit was $400 per person," Mary said, displaying the sort of argumentative tone that just pissed Janice off more. Mary seemed not to have gotten the message: as soon as she expressed contrition, Janice would get off her case.

"No, ma'am. The law changed. It's $800 per person. $1600 per couple."

"It doesn't say that on the form."

"That's the law," Janice said. "If the items in question exceed the limit, we seize them."

"You take the clothes off my back?"

"If you want to put it that way, ma'am," Janice said. "If the total of the claimed items purchased exceeds $1600 for a married couple, additional duty is charged."

"How much is that?" Mary asked.

"One percent."

"That's all?" Mary asked. "That's it?"

"That's correct," Janice said.

"Well, why don't you put that on the form?" Mary asked. "Why do you keep it a secret?"

"You're supposed to tell the truth. You signed a form issued by the Federal government."

Janice Goldwasser was a pissed-off Jewish woman with a gun. This must be what Israel is like, Steiner thought. There are women like this on every corner. Perhaps this is why Steiner had never been moved to visit the place.

"But if you said that on the form..." Mary began.

Janice took her leave as Mary silently finished her sentence, which was basically yet another confession that if she'd correctly understood the law, she would have obeyed it. This didn't wash in Janice Goldwasser's world where the law was obeyed no matter what. Steiner could not help but sympathize with her point of view. Which was likely why he'd taken an instant dislike to Janice: they were very much alike in some ways. Shadow! The Jungian notion of shadow—that which we hate in someone else because it reminds us of what we hate most within ourselves. Steiner had finally incorporated an easy-to-understand version of this idea into his worldview. Mary might be pleased, if she did not accuse him of dumbing down Jungian thought in his TV producer sort of way. Well, it was what he did—and it paid well. Rather, it *had* paid well up until recently.

With Janice Goldwasser gone, Dimitri joylessly resumed his duties with the diligence of an anthropologist who'd stumbled upon a not particularly interesting trove of ancient artifacts. With impressive tenderness, he examined ten days worth of Steiner's dirty sweaters, socks, underwear, T-shirts, stinky running clothes, receipts, and assorted pieces of paper.

"What's this?" he said, holding up the Iraqi bank note with its chilling engraving of a smiling Saddam Hussein.

Oh shit, foreign currency with a picture of the man who was fast being packaged by the government as public enemy number one.

"It's a souvenir," Mary said.

"We met a man who's a journalist who'd been in Iraq, and he gave it to us as a joke," Steiner said.

"Oh," Dimitri said with a smile.

He got the joke.

"Are you carrying a wallet?" Dimitri asked.

"Yes," Steiner said.

"Can I see it, please?"

"Sure," Steiner said, wondering if he'd next be taken into a private room to be strip-searched.

With white latexed fingers, Dimitri unfolded each shred of paper in Steiner's wallet. "What's this?" he asked when faced with the mysteries of Steiner's health insurance card, the instructions for working his answering machine from a remote location, and four unused turquoise tickets for the Paris Metro. Dimitri then removed a stack of three of Steiner's old business cards from the Gucci wallet Steiner had bought in Rome two years earlier, when the price of Gucci in Italy was half what it was in New York. As Pierre had reminded Steiner, that was long time ago. Dimitri slowly read the card. It said Vice President. That was who Steiner used to be, and he guessed that the title might make Dimitri like him less. Steiner thought he might pass for a guy who wasn't that rich with his beat-up jeans, leather jacket, and unshaven face, but the card told Dimitri otherwise.

"Is this where you work?" Dimitri asked.

Maybe Dimitri recognized the logo of the channel Steiner had helped to create. Maybe he'd watched some of Steiner's shows. Maybe Dimitri was a fan.

"I used to work there," Steiner said. "I was laid off."

It felt like a shameless play for sympathy, but it was the truth.

"How long ago?" Dimitri asked.

Steiner sensed that this was a personal, not professional question, but he answered it.

Dimitri nodded sympathetically and handed back the wallet that had cost Steiner a hundred bucks in Rome.

The man who'd taken the passports returned, and eyeballing Steiner with great suspicion, asked to confer with Dimitri in private.

"Can we get our passports back, please?" Mary asked, sounding a bit too pissed off to get results.

"Not yet, ma'am," the officer said.

The thing about breaking the law, even a minor law, Steiner thought, is that you're wrong, while everyone who is on the team that caught you is right. It really was no fun getting caught doing anything wrong, especially for someone like Steiner, who was experiencing this little encounter with a chagrin equal to what most people might feel if caught smuggling five kilos of cocaine and were facing federal prison time. Michael, by contrast, seemed to have endured his twenty-four hours or so in the local lock-up with a very sophisticated, somewhat Parisian nonchalance. Good for him. Michael was better at getting in trouble than his old man, Steiner concluded with a sense of pride and relief.

"What's their total?" Janice Goldwasser asked Dimitri upon her return.

After Dimitri examined the complete collection of receipts he'd found in Mary's purse, he finished his calculations like a guy behind a deli counter struggling to add up the cost of the turkey sandwich, soda, and coleslaw he'd just put in a brown bag: he might be good at making the sandwich, but math was not his best subject. Finally, Dimitri looked up from his calculator and said, "$1532."

No, that can't be, Steiner thought. Mary's illegal Lagerfeld jacket probably cost almost that much. And how much was that Vuitton bag she bought herself? Steiner had not even wanted to know what it cost. Dimitri had clearly made a mistake. Should Steiner correct it? He looked at Mary's face. She had caught the mistake too. Wisely, she did not look at her husband, and though her eyes were focused on the two strangers who were, at the moment, the two most important people in her life, Mary seemed to be telling her husband not to be a goody-two-shoes asshole and just shut the fuck up.

"Are you sure?" Janice asked Dimitri.

Dimitri looked down again at his notes, but he seemed almost to be faking it: his unspoken calculations looked like pantomime to Steiner who, though he presently felt like he might not know much about human life, still knew a bad performance when he saw it.

"They're okay," Dimitri said in a voice that to Steiner felt like a very generous assessment of him and his wife as a couple, as citizens of the United States. In Dimitri's eyes, they were okay. Steiner wanted to hand him a thousand dollars in cash, though Janice would likely frown upon the gesture.

"Well, you still have to pay a fine," Janice Goldwasser said with a disappointed air. Perhaps she'd had her eyes on the Lagerfeld jacket. It might look good on her.

"Your fine is ten percent of what you failed to declare," Janice added. "So it won't be much over a hundred bucks. Is that okay?"

Is it okay? Steiner thought. It's a little slice of heaven. Just give me my passport back and let me pay whatever I need to pay so I can get the fuck out of here. Over an hour had passed since this small ordeal began.

"Thank you," Steiner and his wife chorused.

"We're sorry," Steiner said.

"Yes, we're sorry," Mary said finally. "It won't happen again."

"Don't worry about it," Janice Goldwasser said. "It happens every day."

Taxi rides back to the city from the airport after European holidays were usually fairly silent affairs for Steiner and Mary. It bothered Mary that Steiner always seemed so happy to return to New York and often said something as innocent as "wow" when he saw the illuminated skyline for the first time after even a brief absence. To Mary, Steiner sensed, this seemed small-minded, a neurotic's happiness at returning to the familiar rituals that numbed him from new experiences or deeper issues that Steiner typically chose to ignore in favor of, say, a three-hour sit-down with the Sunday *Times*. But on this night the approach to the city seemed legitimately different to Steiner. For one thing, he was furious with his wife: she had, after all, gotten them into the mess they'd just endured. If she'd listened to him and just told the fucking truth, the whole problem would have been avoided. And the duty on merchandise that exceeded the $800 per person allowance was only one percent. So telling the entire truth would have actually been cheaper than lying and trying to get away with it. And it certainly would have taken less time and been less traumatic.

"Now every time we go through customs, we're going to go through the same thing," Mary said.

"It doesn't matter if you tell the truth,' Steiner said, even though he'd vowed to himself not to rub it in—and even though the whole thing, in his view at least, was entirely Mary's fault.

"But if they'd told us how much we could declare," Mary said, "and how little the duty was… I mean, if I'd known what the law is."

"That's no excuse," Steiner said.

"You would have made a good cop."

"Maybe they have openings at customs," Steiner said. "Maybe I should apply. Janice Goldwasser was Jewish."

"Who's Janice Goldwasser?"

"The supervisor. Her name was on her badge."

"She was a bitch."

"No, she wasn't."

"You're right. She could have been worse."

"Dimitri was fine."

"Yeah, Dimitri was a doll."

Mary tried the cell phone again, finally reaching Michael.

"We'll be home soon, darling," she said. "We're about to get on the L.I.E."

In the silence that followed, the cab driver, a Pakistani, Steiner guessed from the license displayed in the back of the cab, began speaking incessantly on his cell phone. Why was the perpetual sound of a foreign tongue so annoying to Steiner? He'd never confess the irrational hatred he felt at this moment, not even to Mary. That sort of stupid anger was one more thing he really did need to get over. Mary was right: he was a bit of a paranoid, but he was an American; there's no cure for that. He really needed to adjust to the modern world or risk becoming even more of a parody of himself. If he were just a bit more curious, if he could only learn to take the occasional imaginative leap to try to understand what the people he disliked most might be experiencing, it would, at the very least, be an interesting exercise. The same might be said of the leadership of his country, he thought with a smile. Then, as gently as he knew how, Steiner told the driver that he and his wife were very tired and really would appreciate a little quiet.

"Thank you," Mary said to her husband, after the man quickly ended his phone conversation.

"Are we really going to tell Michael about our little encounter with the U.S. Customs service?" Mary asked.

"Of course. He'll think it's pretty funny."

"We can compare cop stories," Mary said. "We're becoming a dangerous family."

"We might actually be the least dangerous family in America."

"I'm sorry," Mary said, taking Steiner's hand. "That was my fault."

Her hand, the feeling of it in his almost always made him deeply happy.

"For once," Steiner said. "For once I was right."

Mary drew close to Steiner and leaned her head against his shoulder. Nice touch, the producer within him thought. How entirely pleasant. She smelled like Mary, which was just one more thing that Steiner could not express in words, and she smelled like the stale air in an airplane, too.

At dinner with Johnny and Claire on the rue Lepic, Steiner had accused himself of knowing nothing about courage, nothing about truth, nothing about beauty. But perhaps he did know a few things. He knew that his wife was beautiful and Lord knows she always tried to speak the truth. Michael had done something courageous, though he had done it for conflicted motives, to be sure. And there was still something beautiful within America, though darkness was falling all around.

"Remember what you said about that dream I had?" Steiner asked. "The one about New York."

"I said it was about hope."

"I don't see the hope."

"Nonsense," Mary said, still leaning against her husband's shoulder. "You have Michael, you have me, you have your health. Years from now you'll look back on this moment and think: 'I was so young.'"

Mary sat up straight.

"Look," she told her husband. "There it is. You have your city, too."

Steiner was briefly content. Up ahead he saw the white lights of his beloved home, the wounded skyline no New Yorker could view without worry or feelings of bitterness and loss.

✦ ACKNOWLEDGEMENTS ✦

I would like to thank a few loyal readers for their comments on this manuscript: Jon Brandeis, Mia Goldman, Paul Golub, Lorraine Kreahling, Bob Lampel, Vicky Lowry, and Gabriella Mirabelli.

—R.K.F.

148